DEAD MAN'S CANYON

by

Robert Broomall

Books by Robert Broomall

Death's Head: A Soldier With Richard the Lionheart
The Red King: A Soldier With Richard the Lionheart, II
California Kingdoms
Texas Kingdoms
The Lawmen
The Bank Robber
Dead Man's Crossing (Jake Moran 1)
Dead Man's Town (Jake Moran 2)
K Company (K Company 1)
Conroy's First Command (K Company 2)
The Dispatch Rider (K Company 3)
Scalp Hunters (Cole Taggart 1)
Paradise Mountain (Cole Taggart 2)
Wild Bill and the Dinosaur Hunters
Murder in the Seventh Cavalry

PROLOGUE—1837

"Looks like we got company," said Harry Denton, gazing to the rear.

Tom Shaw turned in the saddle, as did the rest of the party. A lone rider sat his horse about a half-mile behind them, almost obscured by the shimmering heat haze and the glare of the morning sun.

There were six men in the party, Americans. They'd been on the move since before dawn, to avoid the furnace-like heat of the northern Sonora Desert. They were dressed in coarse, much-mended woolens and buckskins. Men and horses looked thin and wolfish, as though they hadn't eaten much lately. Each man carried a long rifle and a brace of Colt's newly invented revolving pistols.

Tom Shaw was twenty, a cloth merchant's son from Baltimore. He'd been in St. Louis on business when, fired with adventure, he'd taken his father's merchandise and joined this year's trading expedition down the Santa Fe Trail to Mexico. He'd been fresh faced then. Now, five months later, he was gaunt and hollow, his cheeks covered with blond stubble, as he shaded his eyes and studied the distant rider. He could make out few details, save for some sort of spear or lance in the man's hand.

"Soldier," said Denton. Denton was their captain, a square-jawed, square-shouldered frontiersman with long side-whiskers. He was in his mid-thirties, and he had the best eyes in the group. "Likely point rider for a column."

"What's a column of soldiers doing way out here?" said the Tennessee planter O'Neill nervously. They were deep in Mexican territory—at least ninety miles south of Tucson—and since last year's Texas rebellion, Americans found themselves unwelcome in this part of the world.

Denton swung off his horse calmly. "Reckon we might as well wait here and see. Ain't no gettin' away from 'em, not on these nags of ours. Just be sure your guns is loaded. If it comes to a fight, shoot the officers first."

Tom and his friends moved off the trail in a rough arc, bodies covered by their horses. They drew their rifles, loosened the revolvers in their belts. The distant rider disappeared and returned with another, who studied the Americans for a few minutes—the sun flashed off what must have been a brass telescope. Then the two Mexicans trotted forward.

The officer was tall and hawk faced. Tom was impressed with his helmet and its bobbing horsehair crest, with his heavy epaulettes and the yards of braid looped around his shoulder. The officer was probably as surprised to see the Americans as they were to see him, but he did a good job of not showing it.

"*Buenos dias, senores,*" he said, bowing his head. "I am Major Ramon O'Donoju Morales of the Puebla Lancers—at your service."

Denton stepped from behind his horse, rifle cradled in his arms. "Name's Harry Denton. We're traders from Missouri way, in the United States."

"*Americanos*, eh?" The helmeted major's dark eyes examined them, taking in their tattered condition and their well-oiled weapons. He spoke with the voice of authority. "May I inquire how you come to be here?"

"We been to Santa Fe and Chihuahua, but we had some bad luck and lost all our money. Lately we been prospectin' in these hills, but our luck wasn't no better here. Now we're on our way home."

"I see," said the major. "You will forgive the lack of pleasantries, *senores*, but I must inform you that there are Apache Indians in the neighborhood."

The Americans looked at one another. "We ain't seen no sign," said O'Neill. The planter had a florid face, and he wore a straw hat and wide bandana.

"Nonetheless, they are quite close. I have campaigned in this country before, and I learned to sense when the murdering devils are around. Let me offer you a suggestion—let us travel together, for our mutual protection."

The Americans talked briefly among themselves, then Harry Denton said, "Sure, Major. We'll ride with you."

Major Morales sent his point rider to bring up the rest of the column. Relaxing a bit, Tom and his friends moved back onto the trail. "Where you boys headed?" Denton asked the major, as the pennoned lancers appeared in the distance.

"The *presidio* at Tucson. A change of station." The major smiled wanly beneath his elegant mustache. "I do not like it, you understand, but it is something I must do for the promotion. These men are my escort."

Tom watched the lancers approach. There were about twenty of them, led by a young lieutenant and a big sergeant. Their once-shining brass helmets had been dulled with mud to protect them from the sun; their red and white uniforms were torn and crusted with dirt and sweat. Their equipment was in good order, though, and they kept their formation closed up. The enlisted men carried no rifles or pistols. No wonder they want us with them, thought Tom. He'd learned enough on this trip to know that swords and lances were little use against Apaches.

The soldiers were followed by seven mules, laden with bulging rawhide *aparejos*. Bearded, sharp-eyed Bill Thackeray, Denton's partner of thirteen years, studied the animals. "Mighty fancy outfit for a major, ain't it?"

"I am a gentleman, *senor*," said the major, drawing himself up. "I am accustomed to living in a certain style. I shall be two years in this wilderness."

Thackeray looked skeptical, but the hawk-faced major did not give him time for any more questions. "Now, if you will please mount your horses. Believe me, it is not in our best interest to linger."

* * *

Daylight fled the sky in swirling clashes of red and purple and gold as Tom Shaw picketed his horse. Tom had been riding with the Mexican rear guard: he hadn't seen his friends since that morning.

The party was camped below a rise in a wide, forbidding canyon. Atop the rise was a little spring fringed by cottonwoods and sycamores. The lancers were setting their blankets in precise rows, their sabers and lances stacked ready for use. Major Morales had posted extra pickets, and he bade the men build low fires so as not to make themselves targets for the Apaches.

Tom found his friends spread haphazardly around a small fire. The mesquite crackled with a tangy smell. Tom had never quite fit in with these men, save for Mr. Denton. He supposed it was his Eastern ways—Westerners didn't trust a man who'd never cleared his own plot of ground. The men were trying to act casual, but they were having a serious talk. No one paid Tom's arrival much heed.

"I say it's gold," growled the planter O'Neill. He was drinking water from an earthenware jug, and the liquid sloshed down his unshaven chin. "I been watching them mules—been watching their prints. Whatever they're carrying is heavy, real heavy. Ain't but one thing makes deep prints like that—and it ain't uniforms, nor liquor, nor trinkets for no damned Indians. It's gold. Pesos."

Bill Thackeray squatted on his blanket, puffing his pipe, studying the tired lancers without seeming to. He nodded his head in agreement. "Garrison payroll, most likely."

"That's what I've been thinking," said little Dr. Talbott as he pulled off his worn boots. Before becoming a trader, Talbott had made more of a living from cards than he had from medicine. He smiled disarmingly. "All afternoon I've had the most delicious dream—piles of gold and silver cascading through my fingers."

"Nothin' else it could be, 'cept money," said John Johnston, the Cincinnati ironmonger, wiping the day's grime from his face and neck with a wet cloth.

Their captain, Harry Denton, did not join the conversation. He chewed his lip. looking worried.

"What's going on?" said Tom. sitting down. "What are you talking about?"

"Not so loud." cautioned O'Neill, glancing around to see if any Mexicans were listening to them. He motioned Tom closer, "We're talking about them rawhide sacks the greasers are carrying—no, don't look! We're talking about taking them."

Tom stared at O'Neill, then at all of them. He didn't know whether to be scared or amused. "You're not serious."

"Quite serious," said Dr. Talbott.

Tom stood. "No. No—you can't do that. Not after they offered us protection from the Indians. It's not right. It's not—it's not Christian."

"You're wrong there, son," said Bill Thackeray. "Meeting these Mex is a gift from God. A miracle, I call it, after what we been through—storms, prairie fires, Indian attacks. Three of us dead before we ever saw

6

Santa Fe, two more left in Chihuahua with the cholera. There ain't a one of us ain't busted flat."

"We're only within our rights to take the money, Tom," argued Johnston. "Remember what them Mex soldiers done to our boys at Goliad and the Alamo."

"Remember the taxes they laid on us in Santa Fe," murmured Thackeray, more to the point. "Hadn't been for that new governor, we'd have been all right. Still, I won't like shooting these fellows."

"Come on," said O'Neill, "they're only greasers. What's the palaver? It'll be like shooting clay targets. I thought it was a waste of money when Harry made us buy these revolving pistols back in St. Loo, but I'm glad we done it, now. Each one gives us the firepower of five men." He laughed at his own good fortune, then he grew serious. "Let's put 'er to a vote. I say take the gold."

Johnston folded the wet cloth neatly and put it in his hat. "I'm with O'Neill."

"And I," said Dr. Talbott.

Thackeray took a deep breath. "Me, too."

"Well, I've lost as much as any of you. and I'm against it." said Tom. He'd never seen his friends like this before. "Tell them. Mr. Denton. Tell them we can't do it."

Harry Denton rubbed his chin. "I don't know," he said.

Thackeray set his bearded face close to that of his partner. His voice was quiet but hard. "None of us *wants* to do this, Harry. I'm thinking of my family—you think of yours."

Denton squirmed uncomfortably.

Thackeray went on. "We get home, neither of us is gonna have a cent to his name. Everything we had was tied up in them goods we tried to sell to the Mex. With the Depression back in the States, our prospects ain't likely to improve, neither. Winter's coming on. Think about Claire and the kids. Think how it'll be on them without food or fuel in the cold. Little Adam's been real sickly; think how he'll make out."

Denton bowed his head. Tom stared at him, not believing.

After a moment Denton looked up, glancing first at his partner, then at Tom. "Bill's right, Tom. If it just meant losing my business. I wouldn't do it. But I got a wife and kids. I got to provide for them."

The big frontiersman squared himself. Once he had reached a decision, all inner debate was over. He looked around the small knot of men, in charge once more. "We're agreed, then. Once we start this, there's no backing out."

"No, we're not agreed," said Tom, so boldly that the others turned to see if the Mexicans had heard. "You're talking about murder. I'm sorry, Mr. Denton, but I can't be party to such an act. I won't permit it."

Denton stared at Tom from under his wide-brimmed hat. "You been outvoted, son. This is serious business, life and death. You're with us, or you're against us."

Tom swallowed. "And if I'm against you?"

His companions looked at him with grim expressions. They were changed men; he did not know

8

them anymore. Their eyes had an animal-like quality. O'Neill drew his bowie knife and held it up. "This is what happens."

"Can't be no other way," said Denton. "Don't make us do it, Tom. This is hard enough as it is."

Tom swallowed again. He had no doubt they meant it. In a halting voice, he said, "Then I ... I guess I'm with you."

* * *

It was the hour of deepest blackness, just before dawn. Major Morales could not sleep. Never had he felt the danger so close. He paced back and forth, his tunic thrown over his shoulders to ward off the night chill. He wished he did not have this terrible responsibility.

The fate of all Mexico rested with Major Morales and his lancers. In the *aparejos* of their pack train was a fortune in gold and silver and precious stones, drawn from the secret vaults of Holy Mother Church. Morales was taking the treasure to California, where it would finance the return to power of President Antonio Lopez de Santa Anna. The Church believed that only Santa Anna could prevent the Liberal Party from implementing a new round of anticlerical laws—perhaps even confiscating Church land and property. Whatever the major's personal feelings about Santa Anna, he was loyal to the Church beyond doubt. Men of his family had defended the True Faith since the Crusades.

The major and his men had been on the road for a month, pushing hard, taking back trails and dodging columns of Liberals sent to intercept them. In the village of Tubac, on the other side of this mountain range, they would be met by Santa Anna's agents, who would escort them across the desert to Los Angeles. The major had already lost a third of his men to disease and injury. Any more and—

Morales started. A noise—someone was moving around the camp.

There—again. The noise was coming from the *gringos*.

A chill ran down the major's spine. To add to his fears about Apaches and the Liberals, he was becoming worried about the *Americanos* as well. He'd seen their looks; he'd seen them conferring. It took no great mind to understand they were discussing the contents of his *aparejos*. It had been a mistake to let the *gringos* join his company. He should arrest them while they slept—but where would that leave him when the Apaches struck? For the thousandth time. Major Morales cursed the fool who'd sent improperly armed lancers on a mission like this.

More noise. Heavy boots crunched gravel. More than one of the *Americanos* were awake.

Major Morales bent and shook Lieutenant Castillo roughly. Then Morales pulled a brace of horse pistols from his belt. The young lieutenant rose groggily beside him. His long saber rasped from its scabbard.

Shadows loomed in the darkness. Morales cocked the heavy pistols. He hoped he'd remembered to prime them.

He could make out the *Americanos* now—it looked like all of them. Moving toward him.

"*Senores!*" The major's challenge split the night. "What is it you wish?"

No answer.

Then, from close at hand, the *gringo* boy Tom cried. "Look out, Major—they're going to kill you!"

Morales raised the pistol, but before he could fire, a ball from Harry Denton's revolver pierced his forehead.

The major fell with a gaping wound in the back of his head. Lieutenant Castillo raised his saber to slash Denton, but Bill Thackeray leaped forward and shot the young man in the chest with his rifle.

Tom Shaw stood rooted to the ground in horror as he watched his friends charge into the Mexican camp, yelling lustily to buck up their courage. They shot the sleepy Mexicans in their blankets; they shot them as they got up and tried to grab their weapons. They fired their rifles first, then they drew their revolvers and shot the Mexicans at point-blank range. Muzzle flashes lit the darkness. Men and horses screamed.

Most of the Mexicans were killed on the ground before they knew what was happening. A fortunate few made it out of their bedrolls and into the brush. Though wounded, the big sergeant got to his feet. He knocked down Thackeray with a sweep of his huge hand. He grabbed a lance and thrust it at O'Neill. The blade sliced deep into the planter's thigh. O'Neill screamed and clutched his leg. The sergeant pulled out the lance. Before he could strike again, Dr. Talbott placed a derringer pistol against the Mexican's chest and fired both barrels. The big sergeant shouted a curse, staggered, and fell dead.

It was still. Acrid powder smoke stung Tom's tear-filled eyes and tickled his nose. His ears rang.

Slowly the haze lifted. Tom saw his friends staring at the slaughter they had done. Their chests heaved as their fighting lust ebbed. They were splashed with blood and bits of brain and bone. These were men that Tom had lived with for five months, men he thought he knew—and they had turned into monsters.

O'Neill recovered first. He levered himself upright from the cottonwood tree against which he had been leaning. His thigh was pumping blood, but he did not seem to feel the pain. His only thought was for the gold. He hobbled to the lancers' fire and pulled out a burning brand. The others followed him across the camp, where he took his bowie knife in his free hand and slashed open one of the rawhide *aparejos*.

"Let's see what we got ourselves here." O'Neill dragged a heavy, velvet-wrapped object from the *aparejo*. Tom's friends held their breaths, praying they had not done this horrid deed for some spare uniforms and a few cases of brandy. Clumsily, because of the torch and his wounded legs, O'Neill opened the bundle. Talbott and Bill Thackeray helped him hold the large object to the light.

It was a ceremonial mask of Indian design, very old. The demon's face grinned hideously and its shoulders were a series of entwined snakes. It was made of solid gold.

"Jesus," breathed Harry Denton.

O'Neill burst out laughing. "Ha ha! This is better than money! This piece alone will keep us in whiskey the rest of our lives—and we got us seven mule loads just like it. Ha-ha!"

Snarling with lust, O'Neill reached into the *aparejo* again. He drew forth a smaller bundle; eager hands helped him tear off the cover. The object was a chalice. The flickering light from the brand glowed on etched gold; it glinted off crusted jewels. The men whooped with delight.

"What were the Mex doing with this stuff way out here?" asked Johnston.

"Who knows?" said Thackeray.

"Who cares?" laughed Talbott, and they started back into the bag.

"That's enough," Denton told them. "Time to look at the rest later. Let's pack up and leave this place."

The gold-crazed men came slowly to their senses. They were criminals now, a thousand miles from home. If they were caught, they would be shot. "What about the greasers that got away?" said O'Neill.

"Forget them. By the time they come back here—if they come back—we'll be long gone. Leave the wounded, and good luck to them. Reload your weapons and hitch those—"

"Hold on," said Dr. Talbott. "You're forgetting something. Young Shaw attempted to betray us. What do we do about him?"

Tom wiped tears from his eyes. He stared into a circle of hate-filled faces. "I—I couldn't go through with it," he blubbered, begging for mercy. Then he went very cold inside, because he knew they were going to kill him.

"I'll do it," growled O'Neill.

O'Neill drew one of his revolvers. He stepped toward Tom and put the weapon to the boy's head.

"No!" said Denton, pulling down the planter's arm. O'Neill whirled. His face was twisted with fury. "What do you mean?"

Denton spoke with an anguished voice. "Tom acted by his own lights. I know how he feels. God help me, I envy him. I wish I'd had the strength to stand against this crime like he did."

"Don't go getting religion on us, Harry. A man turns traitor, he dies. You said that—"

"I changed my mind," Denton told him. He looked over the men, and the timbre of authority returned to his voice. "Tom lives. He gets a full share of the treasure, too. And I'm his guarantee for it."

O'Neill breathed heavily, Talbott and Johnston grumbled, but none of them challenged their captain's decision. None of them wished to risk his newly won fortune by fighting Harry Denton.

"Suit yourself," said O'Neill at last. He stuck the revolver back in his belt.

14

Tom closed his eyes. He was trembling, and his breath came in short bursts. He hoped he hadn't shown how scared he had been.

O'Neill stared at the blood-soaked gash in his thigh as if he had just realized it was there. Denton said, "Doc, you best look at O'Neill's leg."

"I'll get my case," said Talbott, moving off.

Bill Thackeray poured fresh powder down his rifle barrel. "What are we going to do with this stuff?"

"I been thinking on that," said Denton as he reloaded the cylinders of the cumbersome revolving pistols. Dawn was just showing in the east. "We can't take it any place under Mexican control. The Mex'll know we didn't come by it honest. They'll either take it for themselves or throw us in jail—prob'ly both. I say strike east for the Rio Bravo and Texas. We can sell these things in New Orleans. They don't ask questions in that town. From there we can take passage home by river."

"Sounds good to me," said Thackeray.

"Me, too," agreed Johnston.

"New Orleans it is," said the wounded O'Neill.

Suddenly there was a strangled cry. The men stopped what they were doing. Tom turned just as Dr. Talbott stumbled past him into the firelight. The little man was grimacing and cursing with pain. There was a long arrow stuck in his neck. Another arrow was buried high in his shoulder.

"Apaches," he gasped. "The Apaches have come."

15

Chapter 1

TUCSON, ARIZONA TERRITORY—1866

It was the moment that Jake Moran had dreaded.

Young Bascom had dealt this hand from the bottom. No jury in the world could have proved it, but Jake had seen it. If it had been only him that had noticed, he would have let it pass and dropped quietly out of the game; but he knew the three other players at the table had seen it, too. Worse still, nearly everyone in the room had seen. They were all waiting for the great Jake Moran to do something about it. If Jake didn't act, the news would be all over the West—all over the country—within weeks. Jake would be branded a has-been, a coward, an easy mark. His life wouldn't be worth a Confederate dollar.

Jake wished he hadn't drunk so much Red Dog, the fiery Tucson whiskey. It was only with liquor that he'd been able to endure life these last years. Colonel Jake Moran was a legendary figure of the West, the equal of Kit Carson or Jim Bowie. He was the subject of books, plays, even songs. He was an Indian fighter, a lawman, a dashing soldier—he had been dubbed "the Hercules of the Prairie." He was credited with killing any number of men, and he was the hero of half the schoolboys in America. In every town, in every mining camp that he visited, there was always someone who'd known him before—in the war, in the California gold fields, or even in Mexico, like Jim Dothan, who sat at the table next to him. And once he was recognized, there was always someone like Bascom who wanted to test him. Jake thought he'd finally escaped all the attention by coming to Arizona and prospecting the lonely Santa Rita Mountains with Kurt Schankweiler. Then Kurt had been murdered.

Jake pushed more chips across the table. "Up twenty."

The crowd made appreciative noises—there were over three hundred dollars in the pot. Jake and Bascom were the only ones left in the hand. Bascom had a large pile of winnings before him. Jake had forty-seven dollars left to wager.

Jake sat back in the chair, legs crossed casually. His cards lay on the table; he hadn't looked at them since they were dealt. He was in his late thirties—old for the frontier. He was tall, rangy, and roughly handsome, with reddish-brown hair and a drooping mustache. The backs of his hands and forearms were crusted with old burn scars. He wore a black hat with the brim turned up at a rakish angle. A long bandana was knotted around the neck of his red flannel shirt, and his heavy wool pants were tucked into high boots. High on his left hip was a holster containing a Remington .44 revolver; there was another revolver behind his back.

The afternoon heat in the adobe *pulqueria* was made worse by the crowd of miners, off-duty soldiers, and men on the run from the law who pressed around the table, laughing and shouting encouragement. The air was rank with sweat and tobacco smoke and spilled whiskey.

"I'll see your twenty," said Bascom coolly, "and I'll raise twenty." Bascom was well dressed, polite, slim. Every hair was slicked in place, and he smelled strongly of bay rum. He couldn't be more than twenty-five, but Jake had known trouble was coming from the moment the young man sat down at the table. The others had played with Bascom before, and Jake could tell they were scared of him. Jake hadn't wanted to play cards in the first place, or even to come to Tucson. He needed to win some money, though. He needed to get out of southern Arizona before the same thing that had happened to Kurt Schankweiler happened to him.

Jake fingered his remaining chips speculatively. Would Bascom back down, or would he fight?

Now was the time to find out.

Jake picked up all his chips and tossed them on the pot. "There's twenty, and I'll up you twenty-seven." That was all the money he had left, and the unwritten house rules said you could not bet an opponent off the table.

Bascom counted out his chips. He pushed the neat pile to the center of the table. "Call," he said.

Jake turned his cards face up. "Two pair—aces and tens."

Bascom let out his breath as if he was surprised. Then he laid out one . . . two . . . three nines.

The crowd exclaimed. Bascom gave Jake a condescending smile; probably he thought Jake was too drunk to notice what he'd done. "A well-played hand. Colonel. It's a pity one of us had to lose."

"It's a pity one of us was cheating," Jake said.

Most of the crowd missed Jake's words. Bascom heard them, but he decided to brazen his way through. He reached across the table for the pile of chips, but he jumped back as Jake's bowie knife slammed into the wood just ahead of his outstretched fingers.

With a sardonic grin, Jake said, "You ain't much of a dealer. Bascom. Those cards come off the bottom."

Bascom was off balance. He had expected a confrontation, if there was to be one, earlier—at the start of the hand. He was not prepared for it now. "That's not true. I ... I never ..."

"I'll make it easy on you," Jake said. "Just give us back what we lost. Then you can go."

The three other players at the table—mining foreman Jim Dothan, McQuinn the Irishman, and Reynolds the Colorado River boat captain—were quiet, and so was the crowd. Neither Jake nor Bascom was going to get help from them. Bascom tried to recover. His eyes narrowed and he snarled, "I'm not afraid of you. Your big reputation don't mean a thing to me."

At that moment, from the corner of his eye, Jake became aware of a new presence in the *pulqueria*.

It was a woman.

She was watching the confrontation from the rear of the crowd. She was in her late twenties, slender and erect, with carefully tended blond curls. She wore a sturdy traveling bonnet and a blue caped dress of prewar cut. Jake found himself staring into her soft blue eyes. At first his stare was returned involuntarily, then the blue eyes went cold. She seemed prim and proper—like a governess, Jake thought—though her full lips gave promise of deeper emotions. Beside her stood a strapping youth of about eighteen who wore a black wideawake hat that couldn't have been more than a month out of the box. The two of them looked alike, and Jake realized the lad must be her brother.

What was a pair like this doing in a desert hellhole like Tucson?

The woman unnerved Jake; maybe it was that supremely self-confident gaze of hers. Everyone in the *pulqueria* was staring at her. A woman—especially one with looks and breeding—was a rare sight in this part of the country, where the only females were occasional Mexican housewives or the worn prostitutes that infested the saloons on Maiden Lane and the Wedge. The woman seemed unbothered by all the faces turned her way.

Abruptly Jake rose from the table. "Excuse me, gentlemen. I'll be right back."

The crowd parted as Jake crossed the room. Jake Moran was supposed to be a ladies' man, and the crowd expected a gesture from him. He prayed that Bascom wouldn't have the presence of mind to shoot him in the back. Doffing his hat, he bowed to the woman, smiling.

"Beg your pardon, ma'am, but you'd best step outside. This is something a lady shouldn't see."

The blond woman started to protest. "But I'm—"

"You, too, son. We'll just be a minute in here." Still smiling, Jake took their shoulders and turned them around.

The woman was not used to being touched by strange men. Her temper flared. "See here, you. I have every right to be in here. I'm looking for—"

"In a minute," Jake repeated. Gently but firmly, he led them out the door and deposited them in the yard, scattering the chickens who were feeding there.

"No one is going to be hurt in there, are they?" demanded the woman.

"Not if I can help it," Jake said. He bowed again. "My respects, ma'am." He replaced his hat and walked back into the *pulqueria*.

He returned to the card table, keeping his eyes on Bascom every step of the way. The young gambler sat stiffly in his chair. One hand was in his coat pocket, and Jake knew he had a pistol there. The crowd and the other men at the table moved back.

Jake remained standing. He faced Bascom across the table. His badly scarred right hand reached across his waist to the butt of his revolver. A shaft of sunlight fell through the *pulqueria*'s tiny window, illuminating the pile of chips on the table between the two men.

"Well, Bascom, what's it going to be?" said Jake.

Bascom stared. He was trying to make up his mind what to do. He shifted in his seat. His body tensed, and he held his breath. Jake watched the hand in the coat pocket. When the hand moved, Jake would pull his revolver and shoot.

21

"Go ahead, Bascom—make your play!" Jake kept the pressure on. His own hand tightened on his revolver; his thumb was on the hammer. "Go on! What are you waiting for?"

In that final moment, Bascom broke, just as Jake hoped he would. He broke against the formidable legend of Colonel Jake Moran. Jake saw it in his eyes. The slender young gambler had decided it was better to be embarrassed than dead.

"Take your hand from that pocket," Jake ordered.

Bascom's will collapsed like a house of cards. He fumed with rage, both at Jake and at his own impotence. Slowly he drew his empty hand from his pocket and placed it on the table.

"Take your money," Jake said.

Bascom scooped a handful of chips into his coat. He was breathing hard.

"Now, get out."

Furious, humiliated, Bascom rose. He looked nowhere but at the floor as he pushed his way through the crowd.

As Bascom left, the men around the table erupted. They mobbed Jake, just as they would have mobbed Bascom had the outcome been different. McQuinn the Irishman reached across the table and shook Jake's hand. "By Jaysus, ye drew him out good, lad."

Jim Dothan, the mining foreman, slapped Jake's back heartily. "You was toyin' with him all along, Jake. I knew you was. You always had a sense of humor in the old days. The look on Bascom's face when you stuck your knife in the table!" Dothan laughed at the memory.

Reynolds, the riverboat captain, was grateful. "I was certain that fellow was dealing crooked, but I was afraid to say anything."

"He's been playin' like that for years," cried someone in the crowd. "He's killed three men in Tucson alone."

Jake laughed grimly to himself. He had never wanted to kill anyone in his entire career, though there was not a soul in this room who would believe that. He hadn't dropped nearly the number of men he was credited with, and mostly it had been dumb luck or accident that they had died and not him. Certainly it hadn't been due to his dead-eye shooting.

He poured two fingers of Red Dog and downed it. Then he raised his voice. "Barkeeper! Drinks for the house!"

That set off another eruption. People were talking to Jake, pumping his hand. He accepted their acclaim modestly; probably most of them would have been just as happy to see him dead. He poured another drink.

"Look out!"

It was that woman. Yelling from the back of the room. He smelled bay rum.

He threw himself from the chair, at the same moment as a pistol went off right where his head had been. He hit the floor and rolled as a second bullet kicked up sawdust and packed dirt, just missing him. He came to his knees, reaching for his revolver, thumbing back the hammer. As Bascom swung his small pistol for a third shot, Jake pointed the revolver and fired.

The shot hit Bascom high in the chest, driving him backward into the crowd, sending his third shot into the earthen roof. The young gambler fell to the floor, his weight dragging several men with him. He lay on his back. A horrible sucking noise came from his chest. One leg twitched feebly, and blood welled through his expensive shirt.

Jake's heart was pounding like it was going to explode. Death had missed him by less than an inch. His left ear rang, and a powder burn throbbed painfully on his temple. He wanted to let his jangled nerves calm; he wanted to lie down and let his frightened body shake itself apart.

"The Hercules of the Prairie" could not do those things, however. Jake picked himself up from the floor. He twirled his heavy revolver and replaced it in its holster. The revolver twirl was his trademark—he'd learned it because the newspapers said he did it and people were always asking to see it.

Brushing the grimy sawdust from his trousers, he turned to the woman. She stood in shock, unable to tear her eyes from the wounded Bascom. Probably she'd returned to the *pulqueria* out of sheer feminine curiosity; probably she'd never seen a man with a bullet in his chest. Her young companion was gazing at Jake in awe.

Jake forced himself to smile. "Lady, I don't know what made you come back here, but I'm sure glad you did."

The woman turned the full force of her boiling outrage on Jake. "Please, sir, do not thank me. I had no choice in what I did. I saw this poor man draw his pistol and I felt compelled to warn you. My act was that of a Christian—quite unlike your own."

Jake's smile broadened. "Nevertheless, I'm in your debt. Miss . . .?"

"Shaw. Alison Shaw. This is my brother, Hammond. We have come to this establishment because we were told that here we might learn the whereabouts of a Colonel Jake Moran."

That line brought a great laugh from the crowd. Jake's smile grew wider still, and he tugged his hat brim. "I'm Jake Moran."

"You?" she said. "Oh, no."

Hammond smacked his fist into his palm. "I knew it!"

Alison Shaw looked foolish, but she recovered quickly, drawing herself up in righteous anger. "It had been our intention to offer you employment. Colonel."

"Had been?" said Jake.

"Unfortunately, we must withdraw the offer."

"Allie!" cried her brother.

Alison addressed both men. "We'll have no one in our employ who drinks and gambles and whose principal recreation is shooting people in saloons."

"He was shooting at me," Jake said. "What did you expect me to do?"

The crowd laughed again, but Alison did not share the joke. "Come, Hammond," she said. She took her brother's arm and led him from the room.

25

Jake watched them till they had disappeared through the open door, then he poured another drink and swallowed it down. He wiped his lips and stepped out of the *pulqueria*. He wanted desperately to get off by himself, to find some fresh air, but there was another crowd of men outside—attracted by the gunshots—and they were staring at him, laughing and calling to him.

"Way to do 'er, Jake!"

"Good shooting!"

"What's that make now—sixteen?"

"Sixteen, hell—twenty-five's closer to the mark, I bet."

Jake could not get through the crowd. His knees felt weak in the heat, so he leaned against the awning pole, smiling casually, as though he shot a man every day of his life, which was what many of these people believed.

He watched Alison Shaw and her brother walk down the street, picking their way around a dead mule. Miss Shaw could be attractive if she gave herself a chance, Jake thought. She moved briskly; the boy was pressed to keep up with her.

If it weren't for Alison Shaw, Jake would be dead now, his brains scattered across the poker table. Bascom must have started to leave the *pulqueria*, then changed his mind and doubled back through the crowd. Probably everybody had been preoccupied with the free drinks and hadn't noticed Bascom's return; or if they had noticed, they hadn't said anything—minding your own business was the Code of the West. There were lots of men who'd like to say they were there when Jake Moran got his.

Jake's hands were trembling. He balled them into fists, but it didn't help. His whole body was shaking. Cold flutters turned his stomach upside down. Taking his eyes off Bascom had been a mistake, a big one. How many more mistakes before there was a bullet that did not miss?

He couldn't stand being stared at any longer. He wanted a drink—he wanted a lot of them.

He drew himself upright and raised his hand, saluting the crowd. He reentered the *pulqueria*, where he was welcomed with more applause and free drinks.

"How's Bascom?" he asked.

"He'll live," said a doctor who was bent over the young gambler's wheezing form.

"Barely," added another man.

"That's too bad," said Jake, as though he was disappointed at losing the sixteenth or twenty-fifth—or whatever number it was supposed to be—notch on his gun handle. He went back to the table. There were chips and cards and spilled whiskey everywhere, but Jake kept seeing the soft blue eyes of Alison Shaw. What was she doing in Tucson? What kind of job had she been going to offer him? He had an awful premonition about that woman.

He pulled his bowie knife from the table and put it in its sheath. "Let's clean up this mess," he said. "I want to play poker."

The first hand had just been dealt when two bearded teamsters barged into the *pulqueria,* out of breath with excitement. "Don't put your guns away, Colonel. Your friend de Lacey's in town."

Chapter 2

The *pulqueria* grew silent.

"What you gonna do, Jake?" asked someone.

Jake raised an eyebrow, seemingly unconcerned. Inside, his guts were churning.

Jake was more afraid of Edouard de Lacey than he was of any man in the world. The Frenchman was an expert shot with rifle or pistol, and he was a famed knife duelist. Above all, he was a killer. It was de Lacey who had murdered Jake's partner, Kurt Schankweiler.

All Tucson knew that Jake blamed de Lacey for Kurt's death. All Tucson waited for a showdown between the two men. For the second time that afternoon, Jake felt every eye in the *pulqueria* upon him.

"Two cards," he said calmly, laying out his discards.

Jake had first run into de Lacey back in '50, when the Frenchman had gotten his start in America dealing monte and jumping gold claims on the Feather River in California. Later, de Lacey had moved to San Francisco and, with an Australian named Skeggs, he had formed a gang that specialized in robbery, prostitution, arson, murder— any crime that came to mind. It had been de Lacey's gang that ambushed Jake when he was a mail rider in the gold fields, and Jake's escape from them had become part of his legend.

Ironically, de Lacey owed his life to Jake. The San Francisco Vigilantes had planned to hang de Lacey and Skeggs. Jake had protested forcefully. He couldn't stomach execution without lawful trial. He demanded the criminals be run out of town instead. Because of Jake's already formidable reputation, the Vigilantes had listened to him, and in the end his views had prevailed. De Lacey and Skeggs had been tarred and feathered and sent off on rails. De Lacey had blamed Jake for the tarring and feathering. To a man of de Lacey's pride, the humiliation was worse than hanging could ever be. He had vowed revenge.

Ten years later, Jake and de Lacey had met again, in the Santa Rita Mountains. De Lacey had warned Jake and Kurt Schankweiler to vacate their claim. That wasn't the Frenchman's style—usually he just killed you and took over. "Honor compels me to let you live. Colonel," de Lacey said. "This will not happen the next time we meet, I assure you. All debts between us are now paid."

Jake had wanted to clear out right away, but Kurt wouldn't hear of it. "This is America," the stocky Bavarian had said confidently. "This is a land of law. That French aristocrat cannot order us about here." The next day Kurt had set out for distant Tucson to complain to the territorial commissioner. Jake had stayed behind to guard the claim but then changed his mind and followed Kurt. He was just in time to see his partner ambushed and shot dead by de Lacey. Now Jake was on the run—for his life.

He poured himself a drink as new cards were dealt. Coming to Tucson had been another mistake. He should have struck out across the desert and taken his chances. He kept his eyes on the door, in case de Lacey came for him. Sweat trickled down the inside of his red flannel shirt. He couldn't stay here long. As they watched him play on, the crowd's expectation of an imminent pistol duel diminished. They fell back from the table. Jim Dothan turned to Reynolds the riverboat captain. "That's Jake for you. He moves in his own sweet time. He knows what he's doing—he's making that French bustard wait."

Jake knew what he was doing, all right. He was getting ready to run.

His reputation wasn't worth dying for, and neither was revenge for Kurt. The real-life Jake Moran didn't have that kind of guts. He had to go soon, too, before the crowd brought de Lacey to him.

He had hoped to run up his stake, but with each hand his pile kept dwindling, and he knew it was time to cut his losses. Better to leave town broke than not to leave at all. He raked in his remaining chips and stood. "Excuse me, gentlemen."

Once again the crowd grew expectant as Jake cashed in his chips, but he took his bottle of Red Dog and moved to the bar. He tossed down a couple more drinks to steady himself, then pushed a handful of dollars to the bartender. "Buy for the boys as long as this lasts. I need to use your outhouse."

At the bartender's cry of "Free drinks!" the crowd hustled forward, momentarily forgetting Jake, who sauntered out the back door.

As soon as Jake was outside, he turned briskly up the alley, making for Pat Bond's stables on the outskirts of town, near Camp Lowell. This wasn't the first fight he'd run from. By the time the story caught up to him, he'd make up some excuse for having avoided de Lacey. He'd say he couldn't find the Frenchman, or that he'd gotten drunk and missed him. Maybe he'd say he had been with a woman and couldn't be disturbed—yes, that might work well.

He kept to the back streets, staying in the shadows of the unpainted adobe buildings, trying to avoid attention. Tucson was a small town, all jammed together as if for protection from the immensity of the valley in which it lay and from the blazing sun overhead. Empty bottles and other refuse were scattered everywhere. The corpses of hundreds of cattle lay among the brush and cactus outside town, where they had been dragged after being butchered, and the smell of decaying carcasses hung over everything. Yells and raucous laughter sounded from the saloons and *pulquerias*.

The Bond Transport Company had been recently constructed and had well-stocked corrals. The air was redolent with animal sweat and baking dung. The braying of mules drowned all other sounds. Pat Bond was a burly man with arms like anvils. Jake found him in his small office, locking his safe.

"Come to settle my bill," Jake told him. Pat had been letting him sleep in the stable, with his horse, for fifty cents a night.

Pat's leathery face creased in a smile. He spoke with a rasping voice. "Riding out, Colonel? Where to?"

"Back to California, I reckon."

"Kind of sudden, ain't it? This late in the afternoon."

"Well, you know how it is," Jake drawled, hiding his haste, hiding his fear that de Lacey might be behind him. "The itch come on me." His mouth tasted like wool from too much whiskey. He wished he had some more.

The bill took most of Jake's remaining money. "Lucky you come when you did," Pat told him. "Few more minutes and I'd have been closed up. Leavin' early tomorrow. Gotta go home and pack, get the wife to fix me some food."

"Thought you looked awful happy," Jake said, pocketing his change. "What's up?"

"Got me a job. Guidin' some Eastern girl and her brother to the mountains south of here."

Jake's smile faded. He felt the premonition again. "I believe I met the girl," he said.

"Says she's an ar-kee-oh"—Pat stumbled on the word—"ar-kee—"

"Archeologist," Jake finished for him. He'd heard the word before, though he wasn't sure what it meant. Something to do with rocks, he thought.

"That's it. Says she's from some museum or other back east. Come out here lookin' for Injun remains. She's hired a big outfit. Seven mules, 'long with all kinds of picks and spades. Drove a hell of a bargain, too."

"That's *El Despoblado*," Jake said, " 'the uninhabited land.' You can't guide them there; you don't know this country. You ain't even been out here a year."

Pat chuckled. "Reckon I'm the only one'll take her. She says no other teamster in Tucson'll touch the job 'cause of the Apaches."

"You'd be smart not to touch it, either," Jake said.

Pat waved a giant hand. "Bless you, Colonel. I ain't afeared of Apaches. I fought at Gettysburg and the Wilderness and about twenty dozen other places you could mention. I guess I can show Apaches—or anybody else—a thing or two about fighting." He laughed again. "Anyways, I can't afford to turn this job down. I need the business bad. This is my biggest payday since I opened—damn near my only one. This Miss Shaw says some of these Injun things might be worth money, and she's promised me fifteen percent of whatever she realizes. She seems to know where she wants to go. I don't expect we'll have much trouble."

So that's why the woman had wanted Jake—as a guide into *El Despoblado*. "If I were you, I'd reconsider," he said.

Pat bristled. For all his genial nature, he was a proud man. "And what should I tell my wife and children? That I'm willing to let my business go under because Colonel Jake Moran says I might see an Indian? It's not like you'd be scared of them yourself."

Jake had no rejoinder for that. He furrowed his brow. "Didn't mean to pry into your affairs, Pat."

Pat waved his hand, all geniality again. "Ah, that's all right, Colonel—you ain't the first. Mr. de Lacey was here a while ago, asking about the young lady. I guess everybody in Tucson wants to know what she's up to."

A chill ran down Jake's spine. "Did you tell de Lacey what you told me?"

"And why should I not? Mr. de Lacey is one of the most influential men in the territory. He's always treated me good. If it wasn't for him buying my grain when he comes to town, I'd not have been able to put food on the table these last months."

Jake shook the big stableman's hand. "Well, so long, Pat. Thanks for everything and good luck. Keep your eyes peeled out there."

"I will, never you fear."

Jake went to the stable and saddled his range pony. He tied on his bedroll and rifle. He led out the horse, mounted, and rode off.

He had escaped.

* * *

As Jake reached the western foothills, he stopped his horse and looked back. Purple dusk was settling in the valley below. The first lights twinkled in the adobes, while to the northeast the towering range of the Santa Catalinas glowed fiery gold in the dying rays of the sun.

Jake's conscience was bothering him. He kept seeing the soft blue eyes of Alison Shaw, like Texas bluebonnets in springtime. He thought of Alison and her brother with de Lacey. The Frenchman had an insatiable appetite for women; there was no doubt what he'd do to Alison if she ever fell into his hands. The boy he'd kill outright.

Jake was terrified of seeing de Lacey again—he was terrified of being within fifty miles of him. Yet honor demanded that he warn Alison Shaw away from the Frenchman. She had saved his life; he could do no less.

Slowly, reluctantly, Jake turned his horse and started back to town.

Chapter 3

Edouard de Lacey found the woman and her brother having supper in a restaurant just off the Church Plaza. De Lacey had heard about a beautiful woman in Tucson as soon as he rode in, even before he learned that Jake Moran was in town. In his desire to find the woman, he had allowed Moran to escape. He regretted not killing Moran, but he smelled profit here, and he was determined to have his share—both of the profit and of the woman.

There was a crowd of men outside the restaurant, oafs from the four corners of the world, gawking through windows and the door at the woman inside. The restaurant's proprietor was standing in the doorway, concerned about possible trouble. He moved aside for the imposing figure of de Lacey.

The restaurant was called "Los Carascoles." It was an adobe *jacal*, like every other *jacal* on the street, only larger. The inside was dark and hot. A Mexican in white cotton picked a guitar tunelessly; a scabrous dog slept at his feet. The air was awash with the smell of frying *tortillas*, of *chiles* and *frijoles*. In a decade out here, de Lacey had grown used to these odors but he still disliked them.

The woman and her brother were seated at a small table. The boy was wolfing down a burnt beefsteak; the woman was drinking what passed for coffee. De Lacey's shadow fell between them as he removed his tall silk hat.

"Excuse me—*Madame* Shaw?"

They looked up. They were impressed, as de Lacey had intended they be. Edouard de Lacey would not have looked out of place as a Greek sculpture. He was tall and broad-shouldered, with a noble brow, wavy hair, and liquid brown eyes. He sported a well-tended mustache and imperial. His good looks were set off even more by his black evening dress, with its white cravat and gloves.

"Yes, I'm Alison Shaw," said the woman.

"And I'm Hammond Shaw," said the boy, rising.

The woman was not quite beautiful, after all—her mouth was too large—but she was far better-looking than any woman de Lacey had seen in Arizona. The boy was all coltish eagerness, his every emotion writ large on his face.

"How do you do," de Lacey said, shaking the boy's hand. He spoke in a deep, rich voice made all the more attractive by his accent. "My name is Edouard de Lacey. I own the largest ranch in this part of the territory. That is my beef you are eating, in fact."

"How did you know my name?" said Alison as Hammond returned to his chair. There was a note of suspicion in her voice.

"Mr. Bond, the stable owner, told me." De Lacey flashed his most charming smile, "By now, I believe everyone in Tucson knows your name, *madame*. Your beauty is our community's sole topic of conversation this evening."

She smiled back coolly, and de Lacey could see that flattery was not the way to win Alison Shaw. "I wonder if I might have a word with you both," he said.

Alison indicated a vacant chair. "Please—be seated." There was the reserve again, the suspicion to be overcome.

"*Merci, madame*—it is '*madame*,' is it not?"

"It's 'Miss,' actually," said Alison.

So much the better, thought de Lacey, so much the easier. "Mr. Bond tells me you are an archeologist."

"Yes, I'm on the staff at the Baltimore Museum of Natural History."

"Then we have something in common. As a boy, I enjoyed exploring several well-preserved castles on my father's estates near Tours. As a soldier in Algeria, I had ample leisure to examine the ruins of a Roman fort at El Oued."

"You were a soldier?" said Hammond, finally showing interest in something besides his meal.

"An officer in the Tenth Regiment of Chasseurs," de Lacey said. He had resigned his commission after shooting the regiment's colonel in a duel, but there was no need to mention that.

At that moment, de Lacey's partner, Skeggs, shouldered by the proprietor and entered the restaurant. Skeggs took a seat in the corner, facing the door, watching de Lacey's back—though neither man gave sign of knowing the other. The candlelight shone on Skeggs's shaven skull. Skeggs glanced at Alison, and de Lacey could see that the Australian's colorless eyes sent a chill through her.

Alison turned back to de Lacey. She seemed suddenly glad for the Frenchman's presence, unnerved by the brutal-looking Skeggs. "I—I'm afraid I don't know much about castles or Roman forts. My specialty is American Indians. I've come to this area to look for ruins of the Hohokam, the ancestors of your Pimas."

"You mean the ones who built the canals on the Salt and Gila rivers?" said de Lacey.

"Why, yes." Alison looked surprised that he knew. She was recovering her self-confidence quickly. "I'm hoping to uncover some of their villages in the canyons south of here, near the Mexican border. I hope to find some small pyramids there, or some of the ball courts typical of Mexico, and prove that the Hohokam were an extension of the ancient Mexican civilization and not a development from the north, as is presently thought"'

"Archeology hardly seems the field for a woman," de Lacey observed.

Alison drew herself up straight. "I have never let my sex hinder me in what I wanted to do."

"I'll say," muttered Hammond.

"Monsieur Hammond," said de Lacey, "he is an archeologist, too?"

Alison's features softened as she looked at the boy. "No. My brother simply refused to let me come out here without him."

"It's my chance to see the Wild West," Hammond explained through a mouthful of beefsteak.

De Lacey leaned back in his chair, smoothing his mustache. It sounded plausible. The woman had a scholarly look, and she was of an age at which she should have been long married unless she had some outside interest to occupy her. Still. . . . More than ever, de Lacey's instincts told him there was money in this. She was holding something back; he was certain of it.

The guitar player strummed a languid chord. The heat made Alison brush back her tight blond curls, and for a moment the candlelight caught the bare nape of her neck. Despite weeks of travel, she smelled cool and fresh and exciting. De Lacey felt his pulse beating faster. He leaned forward and said, "This is very interesting, *mademoiselle*, but I have not come to exchange pleasantries. Rather, I have come to warn you."

Alison had heard it all before. "If you mean about the Apaches, Mr. Bond says—"

"Excuse me, but Mr. Bond does not know this country. I have lived here ten years. My ranch is not only the largest in the Valley of the Santa Cruz; it is the only one that has not been abandoned to Apache raids. Without an armed escort, you are unsafe anywhere outside the city limits."

Before Alison could say anything, he went on. "But the danger comes not only from Apaches. There are men in this town beyond the pale of the law. Some of them believe you have money, and there are your undeniable female charms to attract them, as well. No deed is too vile for these creatures of greed. I am reliably informed that they conspire against you even now. I cannot impress upon you too greatly that your lives are in jeopardy."

Alison and Hammond exchanged looks. Then Alison spoke calmly, and de Lacey knew she still had suspicions— he had not won her over yet. "We cannot afford to hire an armed guard, *monsieur*. We spent nearly all our money on our pack train. What do you suggest we do?"

"Return home," said de Lacey, trying to sound as though he meant it. "Now—while it is still possible."

"It is not possible. The museum would not hear of it. Our funds may be limited, but our ambitions are not. We intend to become the foremost institution of our kind in the country. It is only by making discoveries like the one I intend to make south of here that we will grow— and attract donations."

De Lacey shook his head with an admiring smile, "You are very foolish." He kept smiling, looking Alison in the eye, then he sighed as if making a big decision. "In that case, permit me to offer you my services. I have armed men at my command. I am not boasting when I say that I am probably the only man south of the Gila River who can get you where you wish to go—alive."

"Jake Moran could," Hammond said, with a pointed glance at his sister.

"Ah, yes," said de Lacey, "I heard that you saved Colonel Moran's life today. A shame you were exposed to such a vulgar incident, but that is life on the frontier. Personally, I doubt that Colonel Moran could get you much farther than the nearest distillery."

"I had formed the same opinion myself," said Alison, looking at her brother with grim satisfaction.

That was it. De Lacey sensed that the woman was suddenly on his side. The mention of Moran had been the key—a shared attitude toward one of the West's most famous figures. De Lacey almost laughed out loud at his good luck. Had he killed Moran, he might have ruined everything.

"I would accompany you not only out of personal interest, *mademoiselle*." de Lacey said. "Though I certainly find you interesting."

Alison blushed. She was starting to like him, he could feel it. He went on. "As a man of business, I would ask one third of whatever profit your expedition makes."

"There may be very little of that," Alison warned.

"In that case, the pleasure of your company will be reward enough."

Alison considered de Lacey's offer, absently running one of her long fingers along the rim of her cracked earthenware saucer. "Hammond?" she said at last.

"It's all right with me," said Hammond, who had taken his sister's plate and was now eating her steak.

Alison looked at de Lacey, cocking her head to one side as if appraising him. "Very well," she said. "We accept your offer."

"A wise decision," de Lacey lied pleasantly. "You will not regret it."

Chapter 4

Jake dismounted down the street from the restaurant. His heart was thumping wildly with fear. At the same time, the alcohol was wearing off. His mouth felt like sandpaper and his head hurt. He tried to pull himself together even as he wished he were somewhere else. He thought about riding out again. No, he'd have to go through with this—he couldn't live with himself if he didn't warn the Shaws about de Lacey.

He loosened his two revolvers in their holsters and then flexed his scarred hands and fingers. He rolled a cornhusk *cigarillo* and lit it, letting it dangle from his lips as he started up the street. His only chance was to act like he wanted a fight, to keep the initiative. And pray that de Lacey fell for it. He'd deliver his message, then get out of town as fast as he could.

An excited murmur rose from the crowd as they saw the tall form of Jake Moran approaching. They parted to let him through. The restaurant's proprietor took one look at him and fled into the night.

Jake peered cautiously in through the restaurant door. There was Skeggs in the corner, as he'd expected. The shaven-headed Australian was staring at Alison's back, and the expression on his face spoke volumes. De Lacey and the boy Hammond were toasting something with glasses of dark liquid. Probably brandy—de Lacey liked brandy.

"That's good," wheezed Hammond as he drank. De Lacey refilled his glass.

Alison looked at her brother with disapproval—probably she looked at everyone that way. "Don't drink too much. Remember what happened when you had all that beer in Fort Smith," she said.

They hadn't noticed Jake, who leaned against the doorway, hoping he looked casual and unafraid, hoping he looked like Colonel Jake Moran of the dime novels.

Alison sipped from a cup of glutinous coffee. "Tell me, *Monsieur* de Lacey—"

"Please—call me Edouard. I insist."

"Very well . . . Edouard. What brings you to the Great American Desert? You're a long way from France."

De Lacey sighed. "Too true, *mademoiselle*, too true. I have been in your country sixteen years now. At first I mined gold in California, then I joined a filibustering expedition to 'liberate' the Mexican state of Sonora. When that failed, I turned to ranching. It has not been easy, *bien sur*, but with hard work—and luck—I have made a relatively good life for myself."

Jake took a deep breath; it was time to act. He clapped his hands slowly.

The guitar stopped playing.

Skeggs turned first, furious at being caught off guard. Alison saw Jake and showed dismay. Hammond looked excited. De Lacey reacted with curious amusement.

Jake stopped clapping and grinned. The powder burn on his face throbbed. "That's good, de Lacey, real good." He looked at Alison, but her blue eyes avoided his. "Did he also tell you how he steals cattle in Mexico, then brings 'em over the border and sells 'em to the Army? Did he tell you how he and his men rob stagecoaches and ambush prospectors?"

Jake straightened and stepped out of the doorway, tossing away the *cigarillo*. His right hand crossed his waist and gripped his revolver butt. He took a position facing both de Lacey and Skeggs, and his voice hardened. "Did he tell you how he murdered my partner?"

Alison took in her breath. Hammond's eyes were like saucers. The guitar player ran into the back room, followed by the dog.

Jake's hand was sweating on the smooth wooden grips of the .44. He would shoot whichever man moved first, then swing over and try to get the other one before he was blasted himself.

De Lacey remained in his chair, legs crossed, seemingly unconcerned. A smile played beneath his waxed mustache. "I am afraid I am not armed. Colonel."

That was a break if it was true. "Maybe not," growled Jake, "but Skeggs is. Tell him if he makes a wrong move, I'll kill him."

The shaven-headed Australian half rose, his chair scraping the floor. "Why, you bloody—"

Jake started to draw.

"That's enough, Mr. Skeggs," said de Lacey.

Alison looked at de Lacey in shock. Probably she hadn't realized the Frenchman and Skeggs were together. The Australian stared angrily from Jake to de Lacey. Then he sat back down.

Relief flooded over Jake. Then he gripped his revolver harder—now would be the perfect time for them to catch him, when his defenses were down. His eyes flitted back and forth from Skeggs to de Lacey, never stopping. He made himself grin again. "Me and de Lacey go back a long way, Miss Shaw. I was on the Vigilance Committee that ran him out of Frisco in '56. Don't let his fancy manners fool you—he's cold as a snake. He means to kill your brother and take your valuables. When he's done with you, he'll kill you, too."

Alison was staring at Jake in utter disbelief. Hammond obviously didn't know what to think.

The elegant Frenchman affected annoyance. "Please understand, *Mademoiselle* Alison, Colonel Moran is a famous killer. He feeds on his own exploits. I am well known in this territory, so he advances a campaign of slander and lies against me, hoping to goad me into a pistol duel, hoping to add my name to his impressive list of victims. I was in San Francisco, but I was hardly 'run out'—by vigilantes or anyone else. As for Colonel Moran's partner, no one knows what happened to him. For all we know, Colonel Moran killed the fellow himself."

Jake had to smile. The Frenchman was smooth, and the woman was falling for every word. Hammond, perhaps, was more skeptical.

Alison stood and faced Jake, visibly composing herself as she tried to control her anger. "Any arrangements that *Monsieur* de Lacey and I have made are not your concern, Colonel. I wish no trouble here. If you call yourself any kind of a gentleman, you will respect my wishes and leave us in peace."

Jake shrugged. He was happy just to be getting out of this place alive. "Do what you want, lady. I just thought you'd like to know who you're dealing with." He lightened his grip on the revolver.

"As it is," Alison went on, "you've ruined our evening—which I suppose is the sort of thing that amuses you." She turned to her brother. "Come, Hammond, it's getting late. Let us return to the hotel. *Monsieur* de Lacey, will you escort us?"

"With pleasure, *mademoiselle*," said de Lacey, rising.

Hammond poured another glass of the brandy and downed it quickly. He left the restaurant with an admiring look at Jake. Alison walked by in a huff, so close that Jake could smell the honeyed scent of her hair. De Lacey flashed a small, contemptuous smile; then he, too, was gone. The shaven-headed Skeggs went last.

Outside, de Lacey put on his silk hat and forced a path for Alison and Hammond through the muttering crowd. They were muttering because they were disappointed—they'd hoped to see someone shot.

For the second time that day, Jake stood in a doorway watching Alison Shaw and her brother disappear down the street. Jake was trembling with relief—there had been no fight. With unsteady fingers, he rolled another *cigarillo* and lit it.

His warning had done no good. He didn't know why he'd expected it to with a knot-headed woman like Alison Shaw. What should he do now?

De Lacey had obviously ingratiated himself onto the Shaws' expedition. Alison was what the weeklies called a lady in distress—even if she did not know it yet—and in the weeklies, the gallant Jake Moran rescued such ladies with aplomb. To come to this particular lady's aid would probably mean death, however. De Lacey and his men, the Apaches, the desert—the odds were too long.

Instinct told Jake to forget it. Getting himself killed wasn't going to help Alison and Hammond Shaw any. They'd be two people who passed through Tucson and were never seen again. No one could blame their fate on Jake—he'd warned them. Still, Alison had saved his life; that was a debt and it had to be paid. And the boy— once again, Jake saw the look of trusting hero worship on the boy's face. That boy believed Jake was the man the papers made him out to be.

"Hell," said Jake, and he threw the *cigarillo* into the street.

He turned inside. He hoped this restaurant sold Red Dog.

* * *

De Lacey led Alison and Hammond down the street. The heat had abated. It was a fine night, though de Lacey hated it, just as he hated Arizona and the United States in general. He yearned to leave this desert inferno and return to civilized life in Paris. But how? It cost a fortune to maintain any kind of style in Paris, and though de Lacey's activities in Arizona enabled him to live comfortably, he was far from rich.

All this because of a woman. Colonel Fournier should have known better than to bring his young wife to a place like El Oued. He should have known where the heat and the boredom and the proximity to restless young men would lead. De Lacey hadn't even liked the bitch. He'd had no choice but to duel her husband, though. The French Army was no place for an officer who would not fight for his honor.

At the time, he hadn't minded leaving France. With the lunatics of the Second Republic in charge, his homeland seemed to be falling to pieces. Within two years, however, there was a new Emperor, and France was on the way back to taking her rightful place in the world. Had de Lacey stayed, he might have fought against Russia and Austria. He might have fought in China or Syria or assisted at the capture of Saigon. He might have joined the Abbe Hue on his epic journey into Tibet. With luck, he could have been a general by now, decorated and famous, an important personage in the Assembly and the salons.

Instead he was stuck in this desert backwater, being driven slowly insane by the never-ending sun. He longed for fog and drizzle along the Seine; he longed for a blustery gray day in the Tuileries. In North Africa, at least, the utter barrenness of the desert had acted as a hypnotic. This desert was cluttered and ugly. Its predators—man and animal—were more deadly.

He had no prospects of leaving, either. He had vowed never to return to France until he was rich, and he was a man who kept his vows. That silver claim in the Santa Ritas might be worth something, but it would need a great deal of capital to start it up, and investors would be hard to find, given the Indian situation. In any case, it would be years before the mine was producing at capacity, and de Lacey did not wish to wait that long. That was one reason he was so interested in the Shaws. They offered promise.

In the distance, a group of young Mexican men rode to a party, playing guitars and singing. The three-quarter moon had risen, and the adobe buildings reflected its light with a silver luminescence. Behind them, Skeggs cast a long shadow on the street.

"That man Skeggs scares me," Alison said in a low voice, glancing back. "I find it hard to believe such a person works for you."

De Lacey's tone was apologetic. "*Mademoiselle*, if I employ men like our Australian friend Mr. Skeggs, it is because this is a hostile land. I must battle bandits and Apache Indians constantly. At any moment a gunman may wander off the street and try to assassinate me—as you yourself have just witnessed. Out here, a man must do things he does not like—as must a woman."

They crossed the Military Plaza and stopped at the hotel arcade. Behind them, the half-built Church of San Agustin glowed white in the moonlight. De Lacey ran his eyes over Alison's slender form, wondering if her body would glow as whitely when he undressed her. "The accommodations in this hotel are unbefitting a lady," he said. "The 'rooms' are merely cots cordoned off with canvas. I maintain a house in town; you two are welcome to stay with me."

Alison hesitated, perhaps debating the real meaning of his offer. She swallowed. "Thank you, Edouard, but it would not be proper for us to accept. We've spent the last fortnight sleeping in a stagecoach, atop a pile of mail sacks. I'm certain this hotel will prove more than adequate after that experience."

She'd turned him down. No matter—he didn't like his conquests to come too easy. "In that case, I will leave Mr. Skeggs outside for the night. He will make sure you are not disturbed." Smiling, de Lacey took Alison's hand. "*Tu permette?*"

Before she could reply, he raised the hand to his lips and kissed it lightly. "That is called a 'Continental gesture,' " he said, smiling at her surprise. "Good night, *Mademoiselle* Alison."

"Good night," said Alison, breathless.

De Lacey clasped her brother's hand manfully, "Good night, Hammond."

"Good night, sir."

" Please—'Edouard.' "

De Lacey bowed to them and strolled away across the plaza.

* * *

Hammond and Alison watched de Lacey as the shadowy form of Skeggs joined him by the flagpole to receive his instructions. Alison glanced down at the hand the Frenchman had just kissed. By the light of the coal oil lamp on the hotel's veranda, Hammond saw the color rise in his sister's cheeks. There was an unusual note of emotion in her voice as she said, "It's fortunate Mr. de Lacey found us."

"He's all right, I suppose," said Hammond. "I mean, I don't believe he'll try to kill us or anything—Jake Moran must be mistaken about him murdering his partner. I'd still prefer to go with Colonel Jake, though. He'd get us to that canyon if anybody could. Why, Jake Moran was the first man into Chapultepec. He's the man who killed Chief Spotted Deer, the man who shot it out with the Coleman Gang and killed—"

"—and killed all four of them single-handed," Alison said wearily. "Yes, yes, you've recited the litany of his accomplishments a half dozen times since you found out he was in Tucson."

"That's because he'd be the perfect one to guide us. I don't understand why you—"

"Because he's not a gentleman. I only went to see him because you kept pestering me. And what do we find when we get there—your paragon of the West shooting someone over cards. The man's a rogue, Hammond—and he reeks of drink. Do we want someone like that with us? Could we trust him? I think not."

Hammond sighed and said no more. He'd never been able to talk his sister out of anything. When she made up her mind, there was no changing it.

Alison looked out at the plaza once more. "Now Mr. de Lacey," she said. "There's a *real* gentleman."

Chapter 5

The smell of death was sickly sweet in the heat. It was morning, their second day out. They were crossing the Sierrita Mountains, southwest of Tucson.

The smell flooded de Lacey's nostrils, turned his stomach, and made the blood drain from his head. Breathing only through his mouth, the Frenchman spurred his reluctant horse forward to join his point riders, Reyes and Nine-Finger Charley.

Reyes and Charley were halted at a rise in the mountain trail. From this point one could see a great way across the desert, far past the massive, cone-shaped peak of Baboquivari in the distance. Before them a body had been raised on a crude cross of mesquite. The body was recognizable as a man by the genitals stuffed in its mouth, and as a Mexican by the *guaraches*, the rawhide sandals, that had inadvertently been left nearby. Nothing else could be told; even the man's wife or best friend could not have identified him. The old vaquero Reyes crossed himself repeatedly. Nine-Finger Charley touched the thin amulet of lightning-fused pine that hung from his neck. Charley's father had been Mexican, and his mother was Apache, the only survivor of an attack on her band. Buzzards flapped on the rocks around the three men on horseback, impatient to resume their meal.

The heat and stench made de Lacey gag, and he placed a scented handkerchief over his nose. He viewed the tortured body impassively. He had seen worse—he had once done worse to a police informant in San Francisco.

Hoof beats sounded on the rocky trail behind them. "Don't let the woman see this!" shouted de Lacey.

Reyes whirled his pony, but it was too late. Alison and Hammond rounded the bend. Alison glimpsed the crucified body in horror, then the grizzled vaquero grabbed her reins and hustled her to the rear of the column. Hammond remained where he was, staring at the grisly sight as if transfixed. The legends of Jake Moran had not prepared him for this gruesome reality. He choked, then he doubled over in the saddle and vomited down his leg and onto the shoulder of his chestnut gelding.

The Australian Skeggs rode up next, along with the Whip brothers. The Whips were from the piney woods of Texas. Dennis Whip was twenty-four, though his sparse beard made him look younger. He was short and slender, and he wore silver conchos on his hat and big Petmecky spurs on his boots. Dennis had killed his first man for twenty-five cents, but he would have done it for free. He was part of a new breed on the frontier, a man whose strength lay solely in his ability to pull a revolver quickly and shoot it straight. His younger brother, Davey, was tall and blond and mean. Davey's first act on joining his brother in Arizona had been to put a notch on his pistol, too. He'd shot a Mexican goatherd and he'd been all proud of himself, until Dennis had told him that Mexicans didn't count. Davey had been riding Hammond since they left Tucson. Now he laughed at the ashen-faced city boy, who was still spitting gobs of vomit on the ground, but the unnaturally strident tone of Davey's mirth betrayed his own fear.

Dennis Whip stared at the body grimly and eased his Army Colt in its well-greased holster. The Texan wore his pistol low, on the same side as his gun hand. This was different from most men, who wore theirs military-fashion, on the opposite hip, or simply stuck them in the waistband of their pants. Whip's position was uncomfortable—the pistol banged his leg as he rode or walked— but he could pull the weapon faster from its holster, and to him that was all that mattered.

"How long ago were they here, Charley?" said de Lacey. "How many?"

Charley, who had lost the little finger of his left hand in a skirmish with his Apache half-brothers, looked up from the ground. "There are forty, forty-five. They finished with this man yesterday, then they headed southwest."

"That many? Then it's a war party and not just raiders," de Lacey said. "Moving in roughly the same direction as us."

The shaven-headed Skeggs spat through brown and broken teeth. "Reckon it's Chief Cochise?"

De Lacey shrugged. The Apaches had been relatively at peace with the Americans until the U.S. Army had murdered a bunch of this Cochise's followers and sent him on the warpath. "Presumably this is the Apache sign of welcome for travelers to *El Despoblado*," he said dryly.

More of de Lacey's men came up. The ferocious-looking Reese, who was a mixture of black, Mexican, and Comanche, saw the body and winced. Girlish, long-haired Angel tried to curb his frightened horse. McNally, the ex-sailor from Maine, put a kerchief over his face and looked away, swearing mightily, while bearded Caleb Buckner took off his plug hat and stared inside it as if afraid to look anywhere else.

"Get this thing down and bury it," de Lacey ordered the unwilling men. He would have let it hang, but he knew Alison would think ill of him if he did. He turned his horse and trotted to the rear. For the trail, he wore white buckskins with Mexican *botas* to protect his lower legs. He had a soft hat with an eagle feather in the band and a casually creased brim. Around his waist was a bright red sash into which were stuck two Starr .44 revolvers. His Mexican saddle was heavily ornamented with silver.

He found Alison with the *atajo*, the pack train. She had taken off her wide-brimmed straw hat. She was sobbing, biting her lips, comforted by the thick arms of Pat Bond. Beyond Alison and Bond, the expedition's rear guard—big Wabash and Curly Bob Brewster—were halted, rifles out, eyes searching the dusty hills.

Pat was saying, "There, there, lass. Put it out of your mind."

De Lacey dismounted, frowning. "Are you all right, Mademoiselle Alison?"

Alison shuddered. Her pale face glistened with sweat. She composed herself with difficulty, trying to ignore the smell that permeated the hot air. "I'm fine," she said. "I suppose . . . I suppose what I saw was the work of Apache Indians."

"Yes," said de Lacey.

"Is such treatment customary on their part?"

"For those who fall into their hands, I'm afraid it is."

Alison took a deep breath. "One hears stories about atrocities, of course, but I had not supposed they were . . . they were true."

"All too true." De Lacey took her arm gently. "Come, we will bypass this place. Avert your eyes."

Alison put her hat back on, and de Lacey helped her mount her milky white mare. At his suggestion she rode astride, on a McClellan army saddle, instead of sidesaddle. Before they left Tucson, she had stayed up half the night slitting a skirt in half and sewing the sides together to make legs. Because of this arrangement she wore no corset, and the firm thrust of her breasts against her cotton blouse had excited the attention of de Lacey's men. She wore new riding boots that the Frenchman had purchased for her.

De Lacey led her past the spot where his men, with kerchiefs over their faces, were cutting down the Mexican's body. Hammond, pale-faced and shaking, was cleaning himself and his horse.

"Do that later, Hammond," said de Lacey in a fatherly fashion. "For now, keep moving."

While Alison and her brother rode ahead with Reyes and Nine-Finger Charley, de Lacey lingered behind with Skeggs. There was not much that the Australian hadn't seen. His mother had been a prostitute, and his father had been transported from England for stealing a hundred yards of calico, value four pence. Skeggs had left his mother early, and the only other thing he knew about his father was that he'd received a thousand lashes for raising his hand to an overseer. Skeggs had grown up on the streets of Sydney Town, where his favorite amusement had been to get blacks blind drunk, then get them to fight with razors and mutilate one another. Skeggs had been a bush ranger, a pimp, and a common strong-arm man. When de Lacey met him, he was one of the Sydney Ducks, the most notorious criminal gang in San Francisco.

"Right professional job, that was," Skeggs said as the corpse was buried beneath a layer of rocks. "Doubt I'd have done much better meself."

"The Apaches learned about crucifixion from the Spanish missionaries," de Lacey told him. "It was the only part of the Bible story they liked."

Skeggs spat again and turned. "Look here, Mr. de Lacey, me and the lads don't mind 'elpin' you chase your bit o' skirt, but we ain't riskin' our necks for it. If that's all there is to this trip, we're turnin' back now." Behind Skeggs, the other men stopped what they were doing. Some of them nodded.

"Don't be a fool," said de Lacey. "Do you think I'd come all this way for a seduction I could have accomplished just as easily in Tucson? Those two are here for more than Indian artifacts. I'll swear to it."

"Well, you better find out what it is, sport. Quick-like."

De Lacey raised a dark eyebrow. It wasn't like Skeggs to use this tone with him. Around them, the other men looked uneasy, and not just because of the Apaches. Only Dennis Whip seemed unmoved. The slender gunman stared at Skeggs with a small smile on his lips. One hand was hooked over his belt buckle; the other rested lazily by his holstered revolver.

Chapter 6

At the noon halt, de Lacey drew Alison and Hammond aside. De Lacey's men were on guard or resting against the suffocating desert heat. The landscape was an endless wasteland of rock and shrub and spiny cactus. A few clouds sailed in the vast expanse of blue sky.

The Frenchman wasted no time. *"Mademoiselle,* after the terrible incident of this morning, I must tell you that my men are afraid—yes, even hardened fellows as these know fear. Unless they are given good reason, they will refuse to continue this journey. We will be forced to turn back. I need to know why you have come here."

"I—I told you," Alison said. "We have come to search for Hohokam ruins."

De Lacey looked at her.

Alison hesitated.

De Lacey laid a hand on her arm. The feel of her smooth skin sent a shiver through him. It was all he could do not to pull her to him and kiss her. He spoke in a concerned voice. "My dear, you would never risk that poor Mexican's fate for artifacts unless you were mad— and I do not believe you are mad. Your caution is commendable, but you have to tell me your secret sooner or later. If you fail to do it now, I assure you this expedition is finished."

Alison looked at her brother questioningly.

"Go ahead and tell him," said Hammond. His face was just beginning to lose the pallor it had acquired at the sight of the crucified Mexican.

Alison moved away from the camp, so they could not be heard. De Lacey and Hammond followed. There was no shade, no relief from the heat. Alison's nose and forearms were red from the sun, and the sleeves of her blouse were rolled up. Sweat mingled with trail dust on her clothes and straw hat.

Alison looked at de Lacey, cocking her head to one side. "Some months ago, our father died after a long illness—I need not explain its nature. Our mother has been dead a number of years, so it was left to me, as eldest surviving child, to administer what little estate there was. With his will, my father left me a letter. It told how . . . well, here, I have it with me. You may read it for yourself."

From her blouse, she produced an oilcloth packet. She unwrapped the packet, took out several folded sheets of paper, and passed them to de Lacey, who smoothed them open. He noted another, yellowed paper that she did not remove.

The letter was fairly recent, but the hand was shaky, with many breaks, suggesting that it had been composed over a period of time. Toward the finish, it was nearly illegible.

De Lacey began to read:

Dearest Allie,

Many years ago, when I was a young man, I took part in a horrible crime. . . .

The letter recounted the murder of a troop of Mexican lancers and the theft of the fabulous treasure the Mexicans had been transporting. It told of the subsequent attack on the killers by Apache Indians:

Poor Dr. Talbott was dead. We'd lost our horses, and we had the Devil's own time loading the treasure on the mules, with arrows whizzing around us in the dark. It was only the Apaches' lack of firearms that permitted us to escape. We shot our way through them and conducted a running fight up the canyon, during which several of us sustained serious wounds.

As daylight came, it became apparent that we could not outrun our pursuers, being slowed by our heavy burden. Accordingly, we halted and buried the treasure. A stone marker was erected on the trail, and I, being the most familiar with pencil and paper, was detailed to draw a hasty map of the treasure's location—which map I have appended to this letter.

Thus unencumbered, we set off again, hoping to outpace our foes, but it was no use. O'Neill could not keep up, and we were forced to leave him behind. We heard his screams soon after. Mr. Johnston was slain in an ambush further up the canyon. Mr. Thackeray was severely wounded, and he shot himself to avoid capture and torture.

All were gone save Mr. Denton and myself. We were out of ammunition, running for our lives. Mr. Denton was too exhausted to go on, and he slowed down. I stopped to assist him, but he waved me on. "Run, Tom, run!"

I ran. At the canyon's crest, I looked back. I saw the savages fall upon Mr. Denton, I saw him go down. Then I myself was shot, and I fell into a deep gorge.

How long I lay there, I do not know. The Apaches searched for me. Several times I heard their footsteps quite close. At last they gave up. They thought I must be dead. I thought the same.

After drifting in and out of consciousness for hours, I began to crawl from the gorge. I must at least make an effort at saving myself, I thought. I reached the top and kept going. For two days I wandered those hellish hills, burned to near insanity by the sun, until I was discovered by a party of vaqueros.

The vaqueros removed me to their ranch. There I somewhat recovered. From the ranch I was taken to Tucson, thence to Santa Fe, where a kindly merchant arranged my return to the United States and my former life.

For twenty-nine years I have been haunted by the events in that canyon. I still hear the screams of the Mexicans as my friends shot them. I still hear the tortured ravings of O'Neill and the last shouts of Mr. Denton. Nothing—not all the drink I have consumed in those years—can make me forget them.

At first I wanted no part of the treasure that we buried, but in later years my mind has often returned to it. Often I have pulled out my map, now cracked and faded, and dreamed of going there, but I have never been able to muster the courage. Now I am dying, and I will never go back.

I have told no one about the treasure until now.

To whom it may have belonged, for what use it was intended, will never be known. It is there if you want it, Allie.

The sin of its theft has been paid for long since. For better or worse, that treasure is your inheritance—yours and Hammond's.

Do good with it—no one knows better than you how its existence has ruined not only me but our whole family. Try and make amends.

Good-bye, I loved you.
Your affectionate Father

De Lacey's stomach was so tight, he could hardly breathe. Treasure! He had known there was profit in this. If only half what this letter said was true, he could be rich beyond his wildest dreams. He could purchase a title—he could be a count, a duke even, with all Paris at his feet. He could go home.

He rubbed his imperial with his thumbnail, trying to keep the excitement from his voice. "And you never suspected your father was involved in an affair of this nature?"

To his surprise. Alison and Hammond looked at each other and laughed. Hammond said, "The only law I ever saw Father break was the one against drinking on Sundays."

Alison said, "We knew he had come west as a young man, but he never spoke about his experiences."

"There is no chance he was . . . making this up?" de Lacey asked.

Both of them stiffened. Alison's blue eyes grew cold. "Our father was not given to lies."

"Quite so." De Lacey refolded the letter. "Your father's story about the massacres is very interesting. As the name *El Despoblado* implies, the lands south of here are largely unexplored, but the Indians who work my ranch sometimes speak of a *Canon del Muerto*—'Dead Man's Canyon'—in that region. They claim it is haunted. You have the map, I presume."

Alison nodded. "I keep it upon my person, for reasons you may imagine." She looked relieved. "Edouard, I wanted to tell you about the treasure earlier, but I was worried about . . . frankly, I was worried about your men. They seem so rough. Is there not some danger that once they learn about the treasure, they might decide to . . ." Her voice tailed off, and she left the consequences to de Lacey's imagination.

De Lacey took her cool, slender hand and caressed it reassuringly in his own. "*Chere* Alison, you are under my protection. Leave everything to me."

* * *

When the party moved out again, Alison and Hammond dropped back with the *atajo* to tell Pat Bond the real reason for the expedition.

The big stableman, who was walking beside his string of mules, slapped his thigh and laughed. "Do you know, I've always wanted to look for buried treasure, just once in my life. Sort of a dream of mine." He took off his low-crowned wool hat and wiped his forehead with the sleeve of his checked shirt. "Does our deal still hold?"

"Of course," said Alison with a smile.

Pat plopped the hat back on, grinning broadly. "I knew you'd bring me luck. Miss Shaw, first time I saw you. It's this trip'll turn it around for my business."

Hammond was curious. "Why did you come to Tucson anyway?"

"Wel-l-l," said Pat, "I always hankered to come west, to live in the wide open spaces, as they say. When I returned to New Haven after the war, I'd lost all my smithing trade to others. I could have got it back, with all the new factories and such, but I decided if I was ever going to make a move, that was the time to do it. So I packed up Maureen and the kids and headed for Tucson."

"Yes, but why Tucson?"

Pat laughed. "I liked the sound of the word 'Arizona,' and Tucson's the biggest town in Arizona—it's the only town in Arizona, as a matter of fact."

Alison had turned in the saddle. She was looking at the rear guard of Reese and Caleb Buckner, who watched the trail behind them.

Pat appeared to read her thoughts. "Don't worry, miss. Mr. de Lacey will keep that lot in line. He don't want to lose his share of the treasure; you can bet on that. Why, this'll put him and that high-spending wife of his in clover."

Alison's head snapped around. "Wife?"

"Sure," said Pat, giving the lead mule's rump a whack with his prod. "He's hitched to the daughter of a big *hacendida* down Magdalena way. Name's Altagracia.

Pretty name, ain't . . ." His voice grew apologetic. "Oh, you didn't know. I see. I—I'm sorry."

The news seemed to hit Alison like a body blow. She reeled in the saddle, gripping the reins more tightly. Shock and self-loathing filled her face as the color drained out of it. She looked as if she wanted to crawl away and hide.

Hammond stared at her, tight-lipped. He knew she had convinced herself she was falling in love with the Frenchman. He could not keep the pity from his expression. and he knew that hurt her even more, because Alison was not the type of woman who liked to be pitied.

Gradually Alison regained control of herself, and a new emotion crept into her voice—fear. "If Mr. de Lacey misled me about his being married, what else might he have lied about?" she asked her brother.

They looked at each other. Alison had more or less raised Hammond after their mother's death, and they were practically able to read each other's minds. They realized now how alone they were, how vulnerable in that vast desert. Anything could happen out here, and there would be no one to come to their aid if it did.

Pat Bond was watching them closely. He waved a hand with the muscular self-confidence that had made him rise to regimental sergeant-major during the war. "Don't you fret none, miss. If there's any trouble, just you keep close to me. I'll see you through."

Chapter 7

They camped that evening at the western edge of the mountains, just before the trail dipped into a large, flat valley. The air around the fire was tense. There was a growing uneasiness between the Shaws and de Lacey's men.

After supper, Pat Bond went to make sure his pack animals were secure. He'd already grained and hobbled them, but he wanted to double check. "I'll be back in a few minutes," he told Alison and Hammond. De Lacey noted that the stableman looked worried. De Lacey's brown eyes narrowed until they were hooded, like a snake's.

Darkness fell. The desert, never loud at the best of times, grew still. Then the night life came out. The quiet was broken by the desperate scurrying of small animals— hunter and hunted. Far off, a coyote cried. The smell of fried jerky lingered in the air, mingling with that given off by the crackling fire.

De Lacey cleaned his revolvers with professional care. He preferred the Starr not only for its performance, but because it had a European look, different from the Colts so favored by Americans. Dennis and Davey Whip cleaned their weapons, too. Reyes and Charley sat together quietly while the rest of the men joked and played cards and glanced with increasing frequency across the fire at Alison. The Australian Skeggs had not been seen for some time.

Alison and Hammond shifted closer to the fire, as if it would somehow protect them. They looked scared. De Lacey saw them glance in the direction of the picketed mules, wanting Pat Bond to hurry and return.

Suddenly Skeggs materialized from the darkness. No one heard him. One moment he wasn't there; the next he was. He said nothing. His brutal eyes looked briefly into de Lacey's, and he nodded.

With an elaborate gesture, the Frenchman stuck his revolvers in his red sash. He rose. His men rose, too. They moved past the fire, circling Alison and her brother.

"What do you want?" Alison said, standing quickly. Hammond stood beside her, feet planted and fists ready, like a schoolboy boxer, looking to all sides.

"We want the treasure map," de Lacey said. This time there was no charm in his voice. "Give it to us and your lives will be spared."

Alison stepped back, seemingly shocked by the Frenchman's total transformation in manner. Her lips worked, but no sounds came forth.

"The map," de Lacey repeated impatiently.

"You're not serious," Alison sputtered at last. "You can't be." She looked into the darkness. She was playing for time, waiting for Pat Bond to come.

De Lacey turned to Skeggs. The Australian bent and picked something up from the shadows. It was vaguely round and he gripped it by the top. He stepped forward and tossed the object onto the ground. It bounced, then it rolled into the firelight and stopped in front of Alison and Hammond, grinning hideously at them.

It was the head of Pat Bond.

"Now do you believe we are serious?" de Lacey said.

Alison's knees buckled. Her face went white. She swayed as if she was going to faint. Then she glanced at her brother, at the look of horror on his youthful face. For his sake, perhaps, she rallied. With a visible effort, she steadied herself and faced de Lacey on shaking legs. At first nothing came from her throat but gagging sounds.

Then she managed to gasp defiantly, "Is this—is this another one of your 'Continental gestures?' "

De Lacey smiled to himself. He admired the woman's spirit. It made him want her all the more. "The map, *mademoiselle*—if you value your life."

Alison tried not to look at the grinning head. Sweat rolled down her pale face. Beside her, Hammond trembled violently. Alison hesitated, then bowed her head, acknowledging the inevitable. "Very well," she murmured.

Reaching into her blouse, she pulled out the oilcloth packet with a shaking hand. She sobbed as she removed the map from the packet and unfolded it. The paper was yellowed, the pencil marks faded. De Lacey stuck out a hand. His lip curled arrogantly. His men muttered and nudged one another.

Alison looked at de Lacey with contempt. Then, before anyone could stop her, she leaped forward and threw the map onto the fire.

De Lacey's men tried to save the map, but the fire's heat was too intense. Skeggs drew back, shaking a singed hand. The others swore violently as they watched the ancient paper crumble, turn black, and vanish into ash.

Alison turned to de Lacey. Her head was high. "I memorized that map, *monsieur*. There is no other copy. You cannot kill me now; I am the only one who can find the treasure. Do not try to torture me, either. I would die before I revealed the secret to *you*."

De Lacey smiled at her, lazily. "We are not going to torture you," he said. "We are going to torture your brother."

Alison gasped. Hammond brought up his fists as de Lacey's men lunged at him. He hit Davey Whip on the nose, knocking him down. He punched Salt McNally in the stomach, then Reese and Wabash grabbed his arms and pinned him. Davey Whip scrambled to his feet, nose bleeding, swearing, spitting blood from his mouth. Dennis Whip moved in front of Hammond, his .44 Army Colt out of its holster and pointed at the boy's face with the hammer thumbed back.

"No," said de Lacey. The Frenchman had not moved; he still wore the lazy smile. "This is Mr. Skeggs's specialty."

Grinning, Skeggs drew a knife from his belt. It was a specially made knife—straight-bladed, double-edged, powerful—good for both cutting and thrusting. The

73

knife that had removed Pat Bond's head. The handle was fitted with brass knuckles. While Reese and Wabash held the struggling Hammond tightly, Skeggs put the knife to the boy's eye.

Skeggs turned to Alison, waving the knife to illustrate what he was going to do. "First I digs out the right eye, then the left. Then I cut off 'is nose. Then the tongue. Then 'is balls. I like to leave the ears on—so's 'e can 'ear 'imself scream."

Skeggs laughed. "This'll be a rare treat, missy. You'll enjoy watchin' this." He moved the knife point back to Hammond's right eye. He held it very close. Whimpering with fear, Hammond fought to move his head away, but Reese and Wabash held him steady.

"Hammond!" screamed Alison.

De Lacey produced a pencil and a pad of paper. He thrust them at Alison. "Draw the map from memory."

"Yes, yes," she cried, snatching them. "Just take that knife away before it slips."

"First draw the map."

Alison licked her dry lips. Her hands were shaking so badly she could hardly hold the stubby pencil. "It's no use," she pleaded after a second. Her eyes were filled with tears. "I can't write."

De Lacey was out of patience. He inclined his head. "You may begin, Mr. Skeggs."

Skeggs's grin widened.

"Hold it!" said a deep voice.

Everyone turned. At the edge of the darkness stood Jake Moran with a pair of revolvers in his hands.

Chapter 8

Jake covered the gang with his Remingtons. The revolvers were cocked, and his fingers were on the triggers. There were two more revolvers in belts slung across his chest. He'd changed from his red shirt to one of faded blue, a color less easy to see.

De Lacey went rigid. He recovered quickly, though, and assumed his usual imperturbable manner. "Well, well," he said, "if it isn't Jake Moran—the Living Legend."

The powder burn on Jake's temple throbbed with his fear. He wished he had a drink. Probably in a minute he'd be lying on the ground with half a dozen slugs in him. He had to do this, though. Alison Shaw had saved his life; he had to try to save hers and Hammond's. He hadn't planned to move so soon, but events had forced his hand.

Inside the circle of outlaws, Alison's face showed surprise, then hope, at the sight of Jake. Hammond looked exultant, as if he'd expected something like this from Jake all along.

De Lacey went on pleasantly, "I confess, Colonel, we did not expect to see you here."

"Been following you since you left Tucson," Jake said. He grinned, trying to sound tough. "Been keeping my distance. I moved in after dark. I'm just sorry I wasn't in time to save Pat Bond."

"Ah, yes—Mr. Bond." De Lacey raised his eyebrows and looked near his feet, where the stableman's head lay in the dirt. The Frenchman shrugged. "He'd never have been successful out here, anyway."

The Australian, Skeggs, had stepped away from Hammond, as had Reese and Wabash, the better to get at their pistols. Dennis Whip dangled his gun hand. Of all de Lacey's men, Dennis Whip was the wild card. The slender youth's ability with a Colt was something that Jake had rarely encountered before. Pistol dueling had been a ponderous, almost stately affair—a test of nerve and wits and sometimes brute strength. Whip and his kind had made it a contest of speed.

This time there would be a fight. Jake's only advantage was that he had the drop on de Lacey and the outlaws. He'd shoot the Frenchman first and hope to scare the others away. It might work. Jake had seen large groups run from smaller, more determined ones before. It all depended on his getting de Lacey first.

"And what may we do for you?" said the Frenchman.

Jake shifted for a better shot. "Set the girl and her brother free. Then you and your men ride out."

Skeggs laughed loudly. Most of the other outlaws were more respectful of Jake's reputation. Dennis Whip's eyes were boring holes in him.

"I am afraid that is impossible," said de Lacey, smiling.

"Then the first bullet's for you, de Lacey, and it's from Kurt Schankweiler."

From the corner of his eye, Jake saw movement. Before he could turn, Dennis Whip had his revolver out and fired.

Jake was knocked down by a painful blow to the waist. More from instinct than anything else, he squeezed off a shot in de Lacey's direction. He rolled over, realized he wasn't shot himself and came to one knee. He leveled his revolvers and began firing at the muzzle flashes opposite him.

Something plucked his sleeve, and something pulled his trouser leg. He couldn't tell who he was shooting at in the darkness.

He exhausted his first set of revolvers. He holstered them and pulled two more. Ten shots were all that remained between him and death. He fired into the fog of powder smoke. The din was terrific, the muzzle flashes continuous. The outlaws were moving in.

Suddenly there was a bang at Jake's ear. Alison was beside him, firing a carbine she'd picked up from somebody's bedroll. Hammond was beside her, shooting a revolver.

Under their combined fire, the outlaw's attack melted away. "Get under cover!" shouted de Lacey's voice through the smoky darkness.

For a moment there was quiet. "We did it, Colonel Jake!" whooped Hammond. "We did it! "

"Shut up and get down!" Jake said.

Jake moved for cover, partially blinded by the flashes. He stepped into unseen brush. Thorns ripped his leg above his high boots. He swore, pulled his leg from the brush, and found cover behind a rock. He could feel blood dripping down his legs from the thorns.

He lay on his back, removed the cylinders and began the time-consuming process of reloading his revolvers. He saw that his heavy Lone Star belt buckle, a gift of the Texas Militia back in '54, was bent beyond recognition. Whip's bullet must have hit it at just enough of an angle to be deflected, saving his life. The surrounding darkness was split by flashes, bangs, and puffs of smoke as de Lacey's men opened a sniping fire.

When Jake was finished with the revolvers, he rolled over and looked around the camp site. The drifting powder smoke made his eyes burn. Nearby, the Maine sailor, McNally, was sprawled lifeless on his back. Another form could be seen lying in a clump of prickly pear cactus. By the light of the campfire, Jake recognized a Confederate cavalry jacket—that would be Curly Bob Brewster. Someone else was moaning. There was no telling how many more—if any—Jake and his allies had hit.

The taste of failure welled bitter in Jake's throat. Nothing had gone right. He had not killed de Lacey. The outlaws had run, but not very far. It was only through a miracle that he was still alive. He felt Hammond's adulation wash over him, and he cursed himself even more. What little success they had met had come from luck and the effect of Jake's reputation on the outlaws. A quick charge would have overwhelmed him at the start of the fight, but the outlaws must have been reluctant to charge "the Hercules of the Prairie."

The sniping continued. If de Lacey's men pinned them there, they could pick the trio to pieces come daylight. Alison and Hammond were looking for Jake to get them out of this. From the distribution of the outlaws' fire, it seemed none of them were near the horse lines. Jake and the others would have to make a break for it. They'd have to cut out three horses, no time for saddles.

Jake raised himself. Someone fired a pistol very close. Jake fired twice at the muzzle flash and heard a scream. No one else was firing on his side. Hammond didn't know how to reload his pistol. Alison was nowhere to be seen. Probably she didn't have the strength to work the carbine's lever—that, or she couldn't figure out how to do it.

Jake began edging toward the horse lines. He crawled past cactus and weeds, past abandoned saddles and bits of gear. Past a pool of blood. He wished he could put out the campfire.

A bullet hit an inch from his face, filling his mouth with a spray of gritty dirt. He spat it out and scrambled behind a thin screen of brush, where he lay on his back, breathing hard. They must have spotted him.

Bullets clipped through the brush, kicking up sand around him. It was only seconds before he would be hit. He'd have to run for it.

He tensed himself.

From the horse lines came a carbine shot, followed by the thunder of drumming hooves. A woman's shouts rose above the racket. There was another shot, and another.

As the hooves receded into the darkness the outlaws' fire slackened. "They run off our horses!" yelled a panic-stricken voice.

"Come on!" cried another.

There were a few more shots in the direction of the camp, then the air was filled with the yells and shouts of the outlaws as they pursued their beasts through the rugged hills.

"Come back here and cover the camp," de Lacey cried to them.

"Not me," replied someone.

"Me either," shouted someone else; it sounded like Wabash. "I'm getting my horse!"

Jake didn't blame them. A man without a horse in this country was a dead man. They could have ridden the pack mules, but they weren't the kind of men to think of that.

Jake got to his feet. He kicked dirt on the campfire. Alison appeared at his elbow, carrying the carbine. She looked pleased with herself.

Jake took off his hat and threw it on the ground. "You chuckle-headed woman. You done it now."

Alison's jaw fell. Then she stiffened. "Frankly, Colonel, I believe it was a good idea to stampede the horses. It gives us time to get away from here. I'm surprised you didn't think of it yourself."

"I did think of it," Jake said. "But I wasn't going to stampede them horses. I was going to shoot them."

Alison gasped. "You mean—you mean kill those innocent animals?"

"It's a hell of a lot better than having that French bastard kill me. Without horses, there's no way they could follow us."

"Still, it seems very cruel," she said.

"It's a cruel world, lady. Now de Lacey and his men will recover their horses and be right on our tail. We won't have more than three, four hours' head start." Jake paused. "I suppose you had enough sense not to run off your *own* horses?"

Alison bristled. "I am not stupid, Colonel."

From behind Jake, Hammond spoke up. "Give Allie credit, Colonel Jake. Those men had you pinned down. If Allie hadn't run off the horses when she did, they'd have shot you for sure."

Jake had to admit there was truth in what the boy said. He picked up his hat. He dusted it off and put it on, grumbling to himself. "Saddle your horses," he said.

Jake moved through the dark camp, bent low in case some of de Lacey's men returned. He gathered as many of the outlaws' water bags and canteens as he could find. He took a full canteen to the moaning man. It was de Lacey's long-time employee Caleb Buckner. The bearded outlaw was propped against a rock, holding his shattered thigh. He was out of this fight. Jake handed him the canteen.

Buckner looked up painfully. "Thanks," he whispered.

Alison and Hammond hurried out their saddled horses. Jake handed two of the water bags—made of heavy canvas caulked with pinon gum—each to Alison and Hammond. He kept two for himself. Then he drew his bowie knife and slit open the remaining bags. He stove in the wooden canteens with his knife handle; the metal canteens he turned upside down and emptied.

Alison said, "What are you doing. Colonel? Without water, those men will die in this desert."

"That's the general idea," said Jake. "Meanwhile, we're getting back to Tucson."

"No, we're not," Alison said. "We're going on."

Jake acted as if she hadn't spoken. Hammond had Caleb Buckner's revolver, and Jake gave him Curly Bob Brewster's revolver and belt as well. Salt McNally's Dragoon Colt he gave to Alison, to go with the Spencer carbine. "We can't go back the way we come. That's the direction you run off the horses. We'll have to follow this valley northeast, then—"

"I said, we're going on."

While Jake checked their saddle cinches. Alison told him about her father's letter, about Dead Man's Canyon and the treasure.

"So that's what this is all about," Jake said. He snorted. "Lady, you got about as much chance of finding treasure in *El Despoblado* as I got of going to the moon."

"The treasure is there," said Alison, "and Hammond and I will recover it. With or without your assistance."

Jake looked from Alison to Hammond. They were serious.

He ran a scarred hand across his face. Here was the same old problem. He couldn't leave these two by themselves. They'd never make it. "We're going back to Tucson if I have to tie you two to the saddle," he told them.

Before Alison could say anything, Hammond spoke up. "Excuse me, Colonel Jake, but I don't think we *can* go back to Tucson."

Jake stared at him.

"We're witnesses to the death of Mr. Bond. Isn't de Lacey sure to follow us to Tucson and kill us before we can testify against him?"

The boy was right.

"There's something else," said Alison. "Upon our father's death, creditors seized all our family assets. Hammond and I were forced from our lodgings with little more than a few dollars and the clothes on our backs. We are a small family; there was no one to take us in. We sold our remaining possessions to give us money to come to Arizona. We don't have return tickets east; we could not afford them. So you see, we have no choice but to find the treasure."

Jake cursed royally to himself. "All right," he said at last, "I'll take you to this Dead Man's Canyon, but I want fifty percent of whatever you find there—which ain't likely to be a whole hell of a lot."

"Fifty percent? Isn't that a bit greedy, Colonel?"

"Lady, this country was built on greed. Now let's get them mules and get out of here."

Quickly, Jake organized the pack train, thanking God that for once in his experience, the mules were cooperative. Pat Bond's headless body lay in the brush nearby. Jake wanted to give the jovial New Englander a decent burial, but there wasn't time. He harried the mules out, whaling them vigorously with Pat's whip. Then he retrieved his range pony from where he'd tied it earlier.

He helped Alison onto the white mare, then he mounted himself, taking the pack train's lead. They started off. In the distance, they could still hear the outlaws calling and cursing.

"Where do we have to go?" Jake said.

Alison hedged. "According to Father's map, the canyon is some fifty miles down this valley."

"Does de Lacey know it's this valley?"

"No, I hadn't told him yet. I was afraid his men would—"

"We can't ride down the valley," Jake said. "We'd stand out for miles. We'll have to cross, then circle down the next range of mountains. We'll try to throw de Lacey off our trail."

"That's if he even comes after us," said Hammond.

"He'll come after us, all right."

The trail ran downward toward the unseen valley below. They went slowly, picking their way in the moonlight. Jake kept a revolver drawn, alert for any of the outlaws who might have slipped in front of them. Suddenly he felt queasy. He seemed to lose the feeling in his fingertips.

"Hell," he said. He knew what was coming. He felt cold, as if the temperature had plunged fifty degrees. He began to shiver. The shivering grew violent; he hugged himself for warmth. He could barely stay on his horse. He brought the animal to a halt.

"What is it?" said Alison, coming up.

"Malaria," said Jake through chattering teeth. "Picked it up in Panama in '49, on my way to California. Caught it again in the Texas bayous at the end of the war. It's a funny kind of malaria, been coming on me real irregular. It'll pass in a few hours." It was always the same. After the chills would come burning fever, so hot he would feel like his body was on fire. After that, sleep.

He said, "Hammond, take the rope from my saddle and tie me on. Tie me tight."

Hammond dismounted, looking at his hero with a worried expression. "Is there anything I can—"

"No," said Jake. With an effort, he reached into his saddle bag and got out a bottle of Red Dog. He uncorked it and took a deep slug. "I'll be all right. Hurry up, and let's get out of here."

Chapter 9

Jake led Alison and Hammond across the valley toward a range of dun-colored mountains running north and south in the distance. They rode through grama grass as high as their horses' knees, through brittlebush and rabbit bush, through creosote and greasewood. They picked their way past cholla and fish hook, past wide ocotillo and towering saguaro. The needle-sharp cactus spines seemed to launch themselves into Jake's legs with a will of their own. He wished he had some rawhide leggings or Mexican *chaparejos*.

Jake was scared. His neck and shoulders were sore from searching the horizon for de Lacey—and for the Apaches who had crucified that Mexican. Sweat burned the cuts on Jake's leg while the heavy wool of his pants rubbed them raw. The malaria attack had passed, but he knew there would be another.

The first chance he got, he showed Alison and Hammond how to load their weapons. Hammond had a Navy Colt and a .44; Alison's carbine had a "U.S." on the stock. Its owner must have stolen it from the Army or been a deserter.

Alison was cagey about where they were headed. "Three buttes in a line signals the entrance to the canyon. We'll pass a finger of rock that Father called the Needle, then we'll come to the spring. About two-and-a-half miles past the spring, we'll see a window in the rock. The trail marker is right below that. After that, well . . ."

"Don't entirely trust me, do you?" said Jake. "Well, I can't say as I blame you." He didn't care if she trusted him or not. He knew there was no treasure.

Jake's long legs dangled over the side of his shaggy range pony. Hammond said, "Excuse me, Colonel Jake . . ."

"Just call me Jake, will you?"

"Sure," said Hammond, obviously awed to be on first-name terms with his idol. "Thanks. Say . . . Jake . . . where's Sureshot?"

Jake had to laugh. He heard that question all the time. The white stallion Sureshot was Jake's companion in a hundred dime novels. Sureshot was faster than any animal on the prairie, and he was smarter than any human except Jake.

"There never was no horse named Sureshot. That's something some New York writer dreamed up." It was one of the few aspects of his career about which Jake was honest. The public liked its heroes to puncture their legends—a little bit, not too much.

Hammond went on. "That horse you're on looks so small. It's not what I expected."

"Don't let looks fool you, son. This fellow is made for this country. He'll eat anything—mesquite beans, old shirts if he has to. You don't have to pack no corn for him. He can go all day in the heat; he can smell an Apache a mile off, and he won't spook like them high-bred animals of yours."

Hammond was impressed. "What's his name?"

"Number Six was what they called him when I bought him in Texas, after the war. Mostly I call him Bill."

They picked their way down one side of a steep wash and up the other, leading their horses on foot the last part of the way. At the top, Alison took off her straw hat and wiped the grimy sweat from her brow. She shook the blond hair off her neck, affording herself a moment of relief. She looked at the prospect before them, another expanse of brush and cactus through which they must ride.

"It's hard to believe there can be so much vegetation in a desert," she said, dismayed.

Beside her, Hammond, who was in excellent physical condition, was not even puffing from the climb. "I think it's beautiful country," he said.

"Too bad it's not good for anything but scorpions and tarantulas."

"Oh, it's good for things," said Jake, who was secretly glad of the chance to catch his breath. "This'll be fine cattle country, once the Apaches are tame and somebody figures a way to get the beeves to market. There's minerals here, too—mines worth millions, but it'll take a lot of money and equipment to make 'em pay. Least that's what Kurt told me."

"Do you mean Kurt Schankweiler?" Alison said. "The partner you said de Lacey had murdered?"

"He didn't *have* it done; he did it himself. Rode up to Kurt on the trail and shot him down. I saw it."

Jake grew wistful. He seemed to hear the German's laugh again, across a lonely campfire. "Ol' Kurt. Little fellow with a big voice, puffing a carved pipe. Looked like a cartoon brewmaster. He was smart, though. He was a metallurgist, from the Bavaria College of Mines. He was sent here by a big outfit of German industrialists to look for silver.

"I took up with Kurt in a Santa Fe saloon. He could drink this godawful stuff called *schnapps* by the crate. He was headed for Arizona, and I'd decided to take up prospecting again, so we threw in together. He was well-heeled, and he staked me. That was Kurt's money I was playing with in Tucson—what was left of it. De Lacey took the rest off his body."

A day before, Alison would have scoffed at such a claim. Now she could easily believe it. "Did Kurt have a family back in Germany?"

Jake rubbed his stubbly jaw, and his voice lowered. "A wife and four kids. He hated to leave them, but this was a big career chance for him. He was to prospect for a lode and open a mine, then the outfit would send over a director and staff. Kurt might be the director himself, if he played his cards right. Then Anna and the kids would join him here for a few years. 'A few years at the most'— that's what he always used to say. After that he'd go home and build him a big house outside Augsburg."

Jake shook his head sadly. "He was a real cheerful fellow. It never occurred to him that things might not work out the way he planned them."

"Is that why de Lacey wants to kill you?" said Alison. "Because you can testify against him, just as we can?"

"That ain't the important part, not for de Lacey. People laughed at de Lacey when he was run out of Frisco. They threw rotten eggs and fruit at him. Important people, people he knew. Now Skeggs, he was just happy to get out of Frisco alive; but a fellow like de Lacey, he can't live with that kind of insult. It goes against his 'honor'—and de Lacey's got a hell of a touchy sense of honor. Something like that gnaws at his insides, like a secret rat. He can't eat right, he can't sleep right, till it's revenged."

Hammond looked confident as they remounted their horses. "Well, he's picking on the wrong man when he picks on you. Isn't he, Jake?"

Jake looked away. "Yeah," he muttered. He only wished it were true.

Chapter 10

The afternoon was well along when they entered the hills. They watered the mules and picketed them in a secluded draw where there was good grazing. Then they remounted, and Jake led them another mile before halting again.

"Are we camping here?" said Alison.

"Near here," said Jake.

"Why so far from the animals?"

"Mules are apt to make noise during the night. This way, if somebody comes to investigate, they won't find us, too."

They hobbled the horses in a grove of stunted cottonwoods. Following Jake's example, Alison and Hammond picked the cactus thorns from their horses' flanks. They watered and fed the animals. Then they took their water bags and bedrolls and hiked another half mile into the rocks, to a niche between massive boulders where they would be invisible to any but those who stumbled directly onto them.

While Alison and Hammond quenched their thirst and laid out their blankets, Jake gathered twigs and busied himself making a small fire, all the while singing to himself:

"Oh, if the ocean was whiskey, and I was a duck.

I'd dive to the bottom and drink it all up."

The campfire was concealed beneath a rock overhang. Jake placed the twigs on it carefully, one at a time. The fire was hot, but there was practically no flame or smoke. Its presence would not have been noticed twenty-five yards off.

To Jake, Alison said, "All our food was in Mr. Bond's packs. I'm afraid it's lost."

"Looks like corn dodgers and dried beef for supper, then," Jake said cheerfully.

That prospect did not entice Alison. "There is game in these hills. Surely we could . . ."

"Shoot something? Sure, if you want to tell de Lacey and every Apache within a day's ride where we are." Jake took out some coffee beans and began crushing them with the buckhorn handle of his bowie knife. Hammond watched him. "That's an impressive knife," he said.

Jake handed the bowie knife to the boy to examine. Unlike the rigid bowie knives imported from England, the polished blade of this one was highly elastic. The blade was engraved with a scene of a frontiersman locked in battle with a feathered Indian. Their wrists were tied together. The frontiersman wielded a bowie knife, the Indian a tomahawk. It was Jake and Chief Spotted Deer, Hammond realized.

"That's a genuine Arkansas toothpick," Jake told him. "Gift of the State Legislature. Hell, I remember when no self-respecting fellow west of the Cumberland Gap would have felt dressed 'less he was carryin' one of those.

When I was your age, it was what folks settled their disputes with. Reckon Colonel Colt changed all that."

"Why don't you use Colts?" Hammond asked. "They're the most popular weapons on the frontier. Are Remingtons that much superior?"

Jake snorted. "I use Remingtons because the Remington Arms Company gave them to me, along with a thousand dollars, if I'd let them use my name in their advertising. That was just before the war. I still have the pistols, but the money's long gone."

The sun was low. The aroma of perking coffee filled the little camp. "Want some?" Jake asked Hammond. "Get your cup."

Jake took the coffee pot off the fire to cool. From his food kit he produced what had once been a cone-shaped loaf of brown *piloncillo* sugar from Mexico. He broke off two big pieces of the sugar and ground them in the bottoms of the tin cups. He filled the cups half full of coffee, then from his saddlebag he took a bottle of Red Dog. The saddlebag clinked; it was full of whiskey bottles.

"Put some of this in it," Jake said. From habit, he shook the bottle first, watching the red liquid foam.

"Why does it do that?" asked Hammond.

"It's got soap in it," Jake said.

Behind them, Alison almost fainted. Jake went on. "Folks that make it figure people like their whiskey to foam. Soap makes it foam. That's nothing—they put rat poison in the juice they sell to the Indians."

He uncorked the bottle and topped off the cups with the whiskey. He turned to Alison. "Coffee, ma'am?"

"No, thank you," said Alison icily.

Jake sipped the hot, sweet liquid. "Ah, that tastes good after a long ride."

Hammond sipped, too. Hesitantly at first, then more deeply. He said, "I still can't believe I'm actually here with Jake Moran. You know, my favorite picture in the whole world is of you. It was in *Harper's Weekly*, and it showed you fighting the Coleman Gang. You looked just like you do now, except you had on your buckskin jacket and your hair was down to your shoulders. There you were, with one foot on the table top, the other on a chair, pistols blazing from each hand, four or five more stuck in your belt. Brad Coleman was lying dead on the floor, Monte Coleman had just been shot—he was falling backward with his hands in the air. Clell Harris was still firing at you, and Ross Waite had turned tail and was running for the door."

Jake tried not to squirm. If you stood on tabletops to shoot at people, you were going to get blown to pieces. Should he tell the boy what had really happened with the Coleman Gang? No, let him go on believing. Let him have his hero. What harm would it do?

"That's the way it was," he murmured.

The sun dipped below the horizon. The western sky was shot through with red and purple, the darkening clouds tinted gold. Alison watched through the niche in the rocks. She looked from the sunset back across the desert they had crossed that day.

She turned to Hammond. "I know I've criticized the West since we left St. Louis, but I'll admit there is a grandeur to this land—if only in its utter desolation. There's no sign of human habitation, no sign humans have ever passed this way."

In the distance, the brilliant colors coalesced. The sky turned blood red, bathing the three of them in its light. "Good heavens," breathed Alison.

They stood there, transfixed by the splendor. A breeze sprang up, ruffling their hair. Then darkness fell, quickly, as it does in the desert, and the spell was broken.

They sat around the small fire, their backs to the rock. Jake poured more coffee and sugar for himself and Hammond. He added Red Dog to the cups. He passed out rock-hard com dodgers and dried beef. Hammond wolfed them down; Alison ate without enthusiasm. The mules could be heard braying from their distant picket lines.

When he was done eating, Jake filled a *cigarillo* husk with rank-smelling Mexican tobacco. American tobacco cost a lot in Tucson, and he didn't have that kind of money. He rolled the *cigarillo* and lit it with a twig from the fire. "What do you all intend to do with this treasure—if there is a treasure?"

"Hammond's share will be used to continue his education," Alison said, glad for something to take her mind off the food. "He's going to become a doctor."

Hammond drained his coffee cup. He looked admiringly at Jake. "Allie, I've been thinking. Maybe I'll stay out West. Maybe I'll be a scout like—"

"You'll be a doctor, young man, and a good one. You have the brains in the family; you'll not let them go to waste."

Jake wondered if he was supposed to be insulted by that last remark. "What about you, Miss Shaw? What will you do?"

"I don't know. I haven't really thought about it. Perhaps I'll open a seminary for young ladies."

Jake spit tobacco shreds from the tip of his tongue. "Runnin' a seminary—ain't that sort of like being a governess?"

Alison looked puzzled. "Something like it, I suppose. Why?"

Jake nodded. "Just wondering."

Alison went on, "The rest of my share I shall give to the poor—to do good with it, as my father intended. And you, Colonel, your share will be as large as ours together. How will you dispose of it?"

"Well, if there's anything to dispose of, I'll give part of it to somebody as a present."

"Who?"

"A friend," Jake said uneasily. "The rest I'll put toward a ranch in California, up Sacramento way."

Jake poured more Red Dog into Hammond's cup. "I wish you wouldn't do that, Colonel," Alison said.

"Oh, Allie," complained Hammond.

To Alison, Jake said, "I expect you're some kind of teetotler."

"I am an associate member of the Washington Temperance Society, yes. But that is not the reason. Hammond is only eighteen. He's far too young to be—"

"Hammond's a full-growed man," Jake said. "Let him enjoy himself. Time I was his age, I'd fought in three major battles and God knows how many skirmishes. Time my brother Ben was his age, he was dead."

Alison seemed genuinely sorry. "How was your brother killed? Was he in the war with Mexico, too?"

Jake swirled the coffee and whiskey in his mess cup, then drank. "He died outside New Orleans. From camp fever. He never even saw Mexico. Never even heard a shot fired in anger."

Jake splashed more whiskey into the cup. "Ben was eleven months older than me. Me and him did everything together. We made our plans for the future together. Ever since I was born, it seemed like life was me and Ben, Ben and me. We was never apart. I expected that would never end. But it did."

He drank again. "Funny, sometimes it still seems like Ben and me. Like he's right here next to me, only I just can't see him."

God, he *must* be drunk, telling them about Ben. Ben had been the hero. Ben was the one they could have written books about. It had been Ben who persuaded Jake to join the Army. Jake had been reluctant to leave the security of the farm. Ben had been Pa's favorite.

There was silence. Alison seemed touched by what Jake had said. With his burn-scarred hand, Jake picked up the bottle. He poured more whiskey for Hammond and himself, and he sank back.

Hammond had a big grin on his face, and his eyes were unfocused. "Say, Jake, is it true that you once raced a blue norther to your camp, and when you got there the front end of your horse was dead from exhaustion and the rear end was frozen to death?"

"Sure is," said Jake, grinning back. "Hated to lose that ol' horse." They drank more and more whiskey, and Jake told the boy tales of Indians and desperadoes and bloodthirsty adventures, exactly as he'd read them in the stories about his life. He'd told them so many times, he knew them as well as the fellows who had made them up. He was a fraud, and he hated himself for it, but he couldn't stop. It had become a habit, part of his character.

Hammond doubted not a word that Jake spoke. He had grown up on the legends of Jake Moran. Beside them, Alison grew madder and madder.

"You think this is hot?" Jake found himself saying at one point. "I recollect when I was scouting for the railroad survey in '53, on the Colorado River. Why, it's so hot there, the chickens hatch from the eggs already cooked. It's so hot there, you eat your bacon with a spoon. It's so hot, the Indians sit in the river all day long so's they don't roast. They cover their heads with mud balls, and they splash water on 'em to keep 'em wet. Those Indians travel down the river on logs, and when they go by it looks like a line of floating mud balls . . ."

"Enough!" said Alison, rising. Her hands were stiff at her sides. "I cannot take any more. Hammond, this man is a charlatan—can't you see that? I won't have him getting drunk and filling your head with such nonsense. Come to bed."

Jake heard Hammond protest, but he couldn't understand what the boy said. Alison's accusation had been crushing. Alison was the type of woman who made Jake feel inferior. He was in awe of her seminary manners, her education, her way of expecting people to do what she told them.

She had backbone, too. She wasn't going to let outlaws or Apaches or anything else stand in her way. Jake's head was spinning, and a revelation flashed through his brain: *she had more courage than he did.*

Then everything went black.

* * *

Something was sticking in Jake's ribs. It hurt like hell. It was one of his revolvers.

He sat up and opened his eyes. Where was he?

In camp, of course. On the ground. Someone had thrown a blanket over him.

He looked around. Everything was dark: the fire had died. He heard Hammond snoring. It must be the middle of the night.

His mouth tasted terrible. Sticky. His head was thick, and he knew it would hurt in the morning. He had to pee.

He heard a noise. His eyes narrowed, and he became alert. Christ, what was he doing—getting drunk and passing out in Apache country. That was a good way to get yourself roasted alive.

There was the noise again. A rustling—and something else; he couldn't place it. Down below the rocks, in the bushes. Whatever it was, it was large. A man. Noisy, too—not an Indian. De Lacey?

Jake loosened his revolvers in their holsters. Unsteadily, he came to his feet. His body felt washed out from drinking all that whiskey. How could he have been so stupid? He made his way to the rocks.

There was more rustling, a low grunt, then a pop. It was a strange noise, like a cork. Then gurgling and splattering. Silence, then a clink, like bottles hitting. More rustling and another corklike pop.

Jake stood away from the rocks. What the hell? He made his way silently down the small hill to the bushes. He heard the gurgling again, the splattering.

He peered into a clearing. In the moonlight, he saw Alison pouring something onto the ground from a bottle. When the bottle was empty, she set it down in a row of empty bottles.

Jake's whiskey bottles.

As Jake bounded into the clearing Alison picked up another bottle—the last full one. As she tipped it over Jake ripped it from her hands, making sure no drops spilled out.

He faced her angrily; it was all he could do not to hit her. "What the hell do you think you're doing, lady?"

She glared at him with a look of total triumph. "I said before, Colonel—if indeed you ever *were* a colonel—I'll have no man in my employ who drinks. Whatever you do from now on, you'll do it sober. *And so will my brother.*"

By the moon's light, Jake watched his precious whiskey drain into the sand. He held on to the surviving bottle for all he was worth. "I ought to put you over my knee, you—you dried-up spinster."

"Spinster!" Alison was outraged. "I'll have you know I'm only twenty-seven."

"You should act it, then. You should be home tendin' your husband and babies. Not out here, chasin' after gold like a damn fool."

He had hit a raw nerve. Alison was breathing hard. Her eyes were wide. "And you, sir—you should mind your own affairs." She turned on her heel and walked back to the camp. "Good night, Colonel."

Chapter 11

Hammond was shaking his shoulder. "Shouldn't we be going, Jake?"

Jake sat up and moaned. His head hurt, and he felt weak. He could hardly open his eyes. Then he remembered something, and he hastily reached out his hand— the last bottle of Red Dog was still there. Thank God, she hadn't gotten it during the night.

Blearily, he dragged himself to his feet. The sun was already rising. They were getting a late start. He stood still for a minute while his head stopped spinning. His mouth tasted like there was a polecat inside. His stomach was rolling. He wished he had something to eat. but he knew there wasn't time.

Hammond seemed in better shape than Jake, but the tight squint of his eyes gave proof that not all was well with him, either. Alison looked furious with them both. She was pinning up her blond curls as best she could without the aid of a mirror. Just like a woman, Jake thought. Always worried about how they looked.

He shook his head clear and took a deep breath. Then he bent over a bit unsteadily and got his canteen. He poured the brackish water into his throat. He felt as if he could drink a lake dry, and he was still just as thirsty when he put the canteen down. Next he wrapped the whiskey bottle in his spare shirt and packed it in his saddlebag so there was no chance it could get broken.

He took his field glasses from their case. They were good Yankee glasses, made in Hartford; he'd liberated them early in the war. He lay in the niche between the boulders and directed the glasses at the cottonwood grove where the horses were picketed.

"What are you doing, Colonel?" said Alison.

"Seein' if we got company." Jake's throat was so dry that it hurt to talk.

There was no sign of any life in or around the stunted cottonwoods except the horses. Slowly, Jake trained the field glasses over the surrounding hills. When he was satisfied they were alone, he rose.

"Hammond, you and your sister saddle the horses. I'll bring up the mules."

He drank some more water—he was glad he'd stolen de Lacey's water bags. Then he took his Spencer carbine and started back down the trail. It was a long walk, and the sun was already hot. He wanted to lie down and die. His stomach felt awful, he wished he could throw up. His head hurt worse and worse, like it was an anvil and someone was beating on it with a giant hammer. The pain was made worse by his anger at Alison Shaw.

He trudged up and down the rocky trail, sweating in the heat. They should have been miles away from here by now. He heard the mules braying just ahead. He smelled them. Probably they were wondering where their keepers were.

He rounded a bend in the trail and then came to a sudden stop. Before him, an Apache was staring down into the draw. The Apache wore a long breechclout and a wide headband, and his face was painted for war. An old Sharps carbine was in his hand.

Jake dropped silently to the ground. He moved behind some brush. The Apache hadn't seen him. Jake's heart was pounding so loudly he thought the Indian must hear it. His hand was sweating on his carbine. The breath came loudly through his nose.

Shifting his position carefully, he followed the Apache's gaze into the brush-covered draw. There were more Indians down there. They were leading out the mules. They had already killed one of the animals. They had cut the mule open, and they were slicing bloody pieces from the liver and eating them raw. There was a large number of warriors. The tall one who seemed to be in charge wore a beaded buckskin war cap with three golden eagle feathers sewn on top. Maybe that was Cochise. More Apaches swarmed up the draw, talking rapidly among themselves, searching for the tracks of the mules' owners.

Beads of sweat dripped out of Jake's mustache, and he licked them off his lip. Should he shoot this one, and maybe have the chance to get one more before they took cover? Should he reduce the odds some? No, that would only put them onto him sooner, and every second counted.

He inched backward the way he had come. He looked behind him, praying he did not dislodge any rocks and make a noise. He crept back down the trail on his hands and knees. When he got a suitable distance from where he'd seen the Apache, he stood up and ran.

He pounded down the trail, panting for breath, feet bruised in his heavy boots. His head jarred painfully, and the crossed revolvers slammed against his ribs.

He tripped over a rock and fell headlong, but he didn't stop. His lungs were seared. Sweat drenched his wool clothes. He didn't look back, for fear the Apaches were right behind him. He scrambled up hills, crying from the pain, and slid down the far sides, tearing his pants. He hoped Hammond and Alison had the horses saddled.

Cactus ripped his legs, but he paid them no heed. He saw the cottonwood trees ahead. Christ, he hoped the Apaches hadn't gotten there first.

There was no time for caution. He came running up with his carbine ready. He saw the horses. They were saddled. Hammond and Alison were staring at him like he'd gone crazy.

Alison said, "Good heavens, Colonel, have you opened that other bottle of—"

"Apaches," Jake gasped. "They got the mules. They're right behind me. Leave everything that ain't on the horses and let's get the hell out of here."

He held Alison's reins and helped her mount. Exhausted, he climbed into his own saddle, and the three of them rode off.

Chapter 12

The Apaches were between them and Tucson. Their only recourse was to flee south, toward Dead Man's Canyon. They rode cautiously, because of the rugged landscape and Jake's desire not to blunder into an ambush. The horses were nervous, seeming to sense their masters' fear.

Hammond and Alison kept looking behind them. They saw nothing. "Are we safe now?" asked Hammond after a while.

"No," said Jake. He was constantly swiveling his head, taking in the hills on all sides of them. "Apaches can outrun horses in this country."

Jake rode with a revolver in his lap. Sweat poured out of him. His head was exploding with pain. He was thirsty and hungry and scared out of his wits. He kept seeing the Apaches in his mind—primitive-looking, like men from the Stone Age. He kept hearing their incomprehensible tongue. He kept imagining himself in their hands, imagining the tortures they would devise for him.

The trail twisted through the hills. Jake couldn't see more than ten feet ahead at times. The hillsides were covered with boulders, ravines, thick brush. There were literally hundreds of places for an ambush. The clopping of the horses' hooves sounded loud. The dry heat stuffed nostrils and lungs; it was hard to breathe.

The low cry of a mourning dove broke the stillness ahead.

Jake's shaggy range pony pricked his ears. He shook his head, snorting. Jake reined in. The others followed his lead. On one side of them the trail narrowed to a steep incline, which dropped off to a saguaro-filled basin. Jake noted a rocky prominence that projected, fist like, on the other side of the basin.

He looked ahead at where the trail left the precipice and passed through the massive, jumbled boulders of an ancient rock fall. Nothing different than they'd seen the last five miles. Thick brush grew among the boulders and at the foot of the hill. The pony's ears were pointing rigidly now. Beneath his legs Jake felt the horse's heart beating. Jake had a presentiment of danger so palpable he could almost touch it.

"Wait here," he told Alison and Hammond.

He rode forward slowly, scanning the rock fall. His thumb was on the hammer of his revolver. His bridle bits jingled in the silence. If there were Apaches here, probably they would hold their fire. They liked to trap the whole party before springing an ambush.

About a hundred yards ahead of Alison and Hammond, Jake stopped. He looked around. He waited.

He swallowed, his chest rising and falling rapidly. He wiped his mouth with the back of his gun hand.

He started back toward Alison and Hammond, then stopped. Something had moved—in the shadows, behind a jagged boulder. Had it been a rifle barrel? He looked harder. He saw nothing. Maybe he had imagined it.

Instinct and fear told him not to investigate, not to leave the relative safety of the trail. They told him to pretend he hadn't seen the movement and to pray for the best. He looked at Alison and Hammond. He couldn't do that.

He urged the reluctant pony a few steps up the steep hillside. He halted again. It was quiet. He still saw nothing.

A few steps more and he had an angle on the jagged boulder. He looked at its base. There was a softer outline there, huddled.

Jake licked his lips and looked harder. It was an animal. It was . . .

It was an Apache.

Jake pumped a shot at the form and turned his horse. As he did, the hillside around him erupted in gunshots and fierce yells. Long arrows whizzed past him. One hit the cantle of his saddle. An Indian appeared from nowhere and grabbed Jake's bridle. Jake swung his heavy pistol barrel, crunching the Indian's head, and the brave fell away.

Jake reached the trail, yelling to Alison and Hammond and pointing to the distant promontory. "Get out of here!"

The Shaws wheeled their horses and galloped off. Jake reined in. He hated it, but he had to cover them. The Apaches were standing now, shooting at him with rifles and pistols, plying their bows. They started after him. He fired his revolver—once, twice, three times— struggling to hold his frightened horse, wheeling him around. He had to give Alison and Hammond time.

He fired again and again. That was five, and he hadn't hit a thing. He holstered the pistol and drew another. The Apaches were running forward; the first ones had dropped from the rocks to the trail. Jake fired one more shot, then spurred his horse and took off.

He barreled down the narrow trail. He could see where it curved in a gentle slope to the basin. Below him, Alison and Hammond galloped across the basin, leaving a long dust plume in their wake.

Suddenly there were yells, and a group of mounted Apaches burst around the hill in front of him. Jake yanked his pony to a stop so hard he almost lost his seat in the saddle. He wheeled. The first party of Apaches was right behind him. They weren't shooting; they figured to take him prisoner. Their yells curdled his blood.

He turned the pony to the steep incline. Jesus, he was going to get killed. The pony needed no urging, for the wild yells had scared him as much as Jake. Jake kicked the horse's ribs, and the animal launched himself into the air. He landed halfway down the incline, hitting on all fours. Jake leaned back and held on tightly, grabbing the animal's mane. The horse seemed to bounce back into the air, then he landed further down the hill and slid to the bottom on his haunches in a shower of rocks and stones.

There was no time to rest. Jake kicked the pony again, urging him for the promontory. He saw Alison and Hammond dismounting on top. He heard the Apaches yelling above him. They started shooting again.

The pony ran hard, weaving around cactus and brush. Jake prayed he wouldn't step into a prairie dog hole and fall. Jake kept his head low. Bullets buzzed past. He heard horses testing the incline behind him.

A ravine yawned in his path, as if by magic. It was too late to go around. He got lower on the horse's neck. The little horse never broke stride, just gathered himself and leaped over the ravine. As he jumped, two painted figures rose from below him and fired rifles.

The horse was hit. He landed heavily, and Jake let himself be thrown. He landed hard on his back, and the breath was knocked out of him. He had lost his revolver. Through a stunned blur, he knew he was a dead man. The Apaches would be on him before he could get up.

Desperately he sought his feet, but it was no use. Here they came, yellow face and striped face. Their rifles were pointed.

From off to the side came yells and a woman's shouts: "Stop that, you devils!"

Alison and Hammond were running down from the promontory. Hammond waved his two revolvers, while Alison carried the carbine, yelling. "Stop, I say!"

The Apaches turned. Their attention was distracted just long enough for Jake to fumble a revolver out of one of his shoulder holsters.

He thumbed back the hammer and shot the striped-faced Apache as he turned back. The ball hit the Apache's chest with a *thunk*. The Apache grunted, staggered several steps backward, and sat heavily. As the yellow-faced Apache turned, Jake shot him, too. The .44 slug went high and hit the Indian in his painted face, blowing it into a mass of blood and knocking him on his back.

Jake scrambled to his feet, shaking his head, trying to clear it. The striped-faced Apache was still sitting, grimacing, making no noise as was the Apache custom. Jake looked at his pony. The animal was dead. His rifle was caught underneath the horse; no time to get it. The mounted Apaches had reached the bottom of the incline. Their yells were close behind him.

He cut loose a water bag and his saddlebags, with their precious ammunition. He picked up his fallen revolver and ran toward Alison and Hammond, who were covering him. Alison was firing the rifle coolly. Hammond snapped off shot after shot with the pistols, anger and the light of battle filling his face.

Jake joined them. All three turned and puffed up the promontory, stopping every few steps to fire at their pursuers. A charging horse staggered, then went to its knees, throwing its rider. The rest of the Apaches hung back, then sought cover.

Jake and his rescuers reached the top of the promontory and dived behind its rock cover. "Thanks," Jake gasped.

Alison nodded, too out of breath to say anything. Hammond grinned proudly.

From down the hill there was a shot, and a bullet whined off the rock a few yards away. Jake looked and saw smoke from behind a patch of brush. There was another shot from somewhere else.

Jake ducked. "They're trying to pin us down," he said.

"Will they attack?" asked Alison

Jake looked back down the hill. "My guess is they'll keep this up for a while, see if they can flush us out. If that don't work, they'll pull up stakes. We're well armed, and we got a good defensive spot here. Apaches don't like to fight less the odds are stacked in their favor."

"Cowardly brutes," said Hammond.

"I'd say they're pretty smart, myself," said Jake. "This here's a war party. They're out to revenge dead brothers. They got a particular target to hit—could be somebody's *rancho*, or one of the big mines around Altar, or another tribe of Indians. We ain't worth much to them, we only got two horses left. They ain't going to wait around for small game like us."

"So what do we do?" said Alison.

"Sit tight. And hope de Lacey don't show up."

They waited. The sun rose in the sky. It beat down on them. They quenched their thirst from the water bags. They spread out, forming a perimeter along three sides of the promontory. Jake was at the low front of the promontory, the direction from which an attack was most likely to come. Alison was above him and to his left, with a clear field of fire. Hammond was well hidden in the rocks on the promontory's heights. Their backs were covered by a cliff. The horses were tied to a juniper pine in a depression behind them.

The sniping gradually stopped. The desert grew quiet, and the silence was worse than the gunfire had been. Once Jake saw an Apache making hand signals in the brush below him. He thought he had guessed wrong, and the Apaches were going to make a rush after all. He nerved himself up, but nothing happened.

An hour passed, another. The oppressive heat made the tired travelers drowsy. Jake found himself nodding off, despite the danger. Then he heard himself snoring, and he wondered if that meant he was asleep. He tucked his head against his shoulder.

A noise. Jake came to, frantically shaking himself awake. To his right a half -dozen Apaches had slipped through the rocks. They were moving toward him.

Jake fired a wild shot. The Apaches yelled and burst forward, shooting. Jake got up and ran back to Alison, who had also been taken unawares. He reached her and turned. The Indians were right behind him.

The only one not taken off guard was Hammond. As the Apaches ran past his hiding place, the young man began firing his revolvers into them. One Indian spun and fell. Hammond fired again, yelling with excitement. He mounted the rocks for a better shot.

"Hammond—get down!" shouted Jake.

Hammond paid no attention. He stood atop the rocks, firing into the confused Apaches. Another Apache fell. A third screamed and gripped a shattered elbow. Jake shot a fourth.

The survivors ran away. One of them turned back and fired his rifle at Hammond, who fell from the rocks, clutching his stomach.

Chapter 13

" 'Ere, go easy on that water, mate." Skeggs grabbed the crudely painted Mexican gourd from Wabash's hands and hooked it back onto his own saddle.

The outlaws were resting, sharing what little water they had left. They were lost in the sun-baked mountain's. It had taken them a long time to recover their horses. They'd had to bury Caleb Buckner, too, after de Lacey put him out of his misery. They were tired and dirty, bleeding from cactus and thorn. They stank of sweat. Wabash, the heaviest, suffered most from the heat. "If we don't find water by tomorrow, we'll be drinking horse piss," he said.

"Yeah, but what will the horses drink?" joked Angel, gritting his teeth against a twinge of pain. Angel had been shot in the arm; the *vaquero* Reyes had made a sling for him. Angel shook out his long, greasy hair. Up close, his girlish features did not look so pretty.

De Lacey spoke to his men with forced cheerfulness, licking his cracked lips. "There is nothing to worry about, *mes amis*. We can squeeze water from the cactus if we must." *Mon Dieu*, these spoiled Yankees. They were like children, always complaining when things did not go exactly their way.

"It's Moran's fault," swore Dennis Whip, the Texas gunman. "I can't wait to get the sonofabitch in my sights again." Whip still could not believe he'd missed Moran with that first shot. He thought he'd drilled the bastard dead center. After that, Whip had spooked and backed off with the others. Now he had recovered his nerve. He was more determined to get Moran than ever. Killing Jake Moran would make Whip's reputation for all time. All he wanted was another chance.

Beside Dennis, his tall blond brother, Davey, nodded in agreement. Davey was content to let Dennis have Jake Moran. Davey intended to repay Hammond for the bloody nose.

"Better find Moran's trail before you start plannin' what you'll do to 'im." said the Australian. Skeggs spat, and he looked at Nine-Finger Charley. So did the others.

Charley was by himself. He squatted, Apache-fashion, eating a handful of parched corn from a buckskin bag. He showed no emotion.

Skeggs went on. "You're part Apache, Charley. Nobody never 'eard of no Apache losin' a trail."

Charley made no reply. He must have known great shame, but he did not show it.

Skeggs said, "You sure you don't know where this Dead Man's Canyon is?"

Charley said, "My mother told me the stories. She had never been to the canyon. I asked the men of my clan at the time where it was, but they—they would not tell me."

"All the same, it seems queer you don't know. I tell you, I wouldn't be surprised if you lost Moran's trail on purpose. You been complainin' ever since we learned about the treasure."

Charley stood. He was proud. "What I said before, I still believe. We must stay away from *El Canon del Muerto*. If we go there, we will anger further the Mountain Spirit who lives there. We will bring tragedy on ourselves. The loss of our water, the death of our friends—these are omens the Mountain Spirit sends us, to warn us away."

"Bullshit," said Skeggs.

Dennis Whip drawled, "Sounds to me like y'all ain't got the guts for this kind of work, breed."

Charley's dark expression did not change. "Perhaps you would care to test my courage?"

Whip smiled. He straightened from his slouch. He unhooked his thumb from his gunbelt, and he poised his right hand by the pistol butt. "If I do, boy, you'll be one dead breed."

The outlaws grew tense. The ones who had been sitting stood hastily, and they all backed away. The silver conchos on Whip's hat flashed in the sun. De Lacey remembered Whip as he'd first appeared in Arizona—his clothes girt with rawhide, boots worn through, wearing a shapeless wool hat. All he'd had was the Army Colt, and he'd used that Colt to make himself a place in de Lacey's organization second only to that of Skeggs. De Lacey doubted that Skeggs even realized he had competition from the slender gunman.

"Enough, enough." De Lacey stepped between Charley and Whip. "We have a bad situation here. Let us not make it worse by quarreling among ourselves."

"Bloody well right it's a bad spot," said Skeggs. "We wouldn't be in it, neither, if it wasn't for you."

Everyone looked. Skeggs hesitated, then he confronted his employer boldly. "I wanted to find out what that girl was up to when we was still in Tucson. But no, you says. Wait awhile, *you* says. Wait while we ride out in the desert and I play fancy man to my little tart. Well, what's come of all our waiting? Eh? We've lost the treasure map, we've lost the girl's trail; and if we don't find water soon, we'll bloody well lose our lives as well. I reckon we waited too long—what do you reckon, sport?"

Skeggs's sudden boldness did not surprise de Lacey. He'd been expecting it. The Australian was restless after fifteen years of taking orders. He wanted to be his own boss.

Some of the men—Wabash, Angel, Reese—grumbled their approval at Skeggs's words. De Lacey plotted the odds in a fight. Charley was loyal; so was Reyes. De Lacey wasn't sure which way the Whips would go. It was important to have them on his side.

Above all, a situation like this couldn't be allowed to fester. It must be brought to a head. The longer you waited with mutineers, the less chance you had of success. The Marquis de Pindrey had tried to outwait de Lacey during the Sonora filibuster, and de Lacey had murdered him. He would have to goad Skeggs into action before any more men came over to the Australian's side.

De Lacey spoke coldly. "If you recall, Mr. Skeggs, it was due to your urging that we moved on the girl and her brother the other night. Had we continued to wait, as I proposed, our rear guard would eventually have spotted Moran trailing us. We would have killed him and avoided this fiasco. If anyone is to blame for our condition, it is you."

Skeggs was about to say something when they heard the distant pop of a pistol. The single shot was followed by a fusillade.

Everyone turned. The shots continued, singly and in small volleys, from pistols and rifles. Skeggs grinned at de Lacey; he was obviously willing to postpone the inevitable. The Australian turned to Nine-Finger Charley. "Well, Charley, this is your lucky day. The *real* Apaches have done your work for you. They found Moran." He jammed his hat on his shaven head. "Right. Lads—on your 'orses. No time to waste."

"No," said de Lacey. The Frenchman ignored the distant gunfire. "There is no hurry." He had to stop Skeggs now. France, money, revenge against Moran and Alison Shaw—all these things were within his grasp. He did not intend to lose them.

Long-haired Angel turned, uncomprehending. "We got to go now, ain't we, Mr. de Lacey? What if the girl gets killed? She's the only one who knows where the treasure is. It'll be gone forever."

"No," de Lacey repeated. "The shots are too far off. We would arrive too late to influence the outcome of this battle, and it is stupid to risk our lives with the Apaches if we do not have to. Colonel Moran is known as a resourceful man; let us trust that he and his friends will win through. If they do, let us not put them on guard against us more than they are now. That way they will grow careless, and we may take them."

Skeggs fixed his brutal features on de Lacey. "I don't think you understand, Frenchy—we're tired of your orders."

It was the first time Skeggs had called de Lacey "Frenchy." He went on. "Ten years I been waitin' for you to get us back like we was in Frisco. But you ain't done it. You ain't even come close. I reckon you lost your touch." He looked at the other outlaws. "I promise you, lads, you'll soon 'ave a copy of that treasure map in your 'ands. I'll make that bitch talk. And when she's done talking, you'll 'ave 'er, too."

The mention of Alison excited the men. Some of them had not had a woman in months. Only two showed no reaction: Charley and Reyes. Reyes stood munching a fiery red *chilipiquin* pepper, as was his habit even in this torrid heat. Nobody knew how old the grizzled *vaquero* was. He'd worked the ranches in the Santa Cruz Valley since anyone could remember. He came from someplace down south, they said, near the Mexican capital. He dressed plainly, unlike a lot of *vaqueros*, and there was a hint of the soldier in his stiff-backed posture. He was inquisitive in a quiet way, as if constantly searching for something.

Skeggs turned back to de Lacey. The Australian grinned, revealing his rotten teeth. "I want that bitch so bad, I can taste 'er. That's a real lady, that is. With a bit o' prodding, I bet she'll perform better'n' a Frisco 'ore. I bet she'll even be better than that doctor's wife I kidnapped back in '55." He laughed at the memory and turned. "What say, lads? Everybody gets as many goes at 'er as 'e wants!"

De Lacey interrupted the resultant hooting and laughter. "No one touches that woman until I say."

"Wrong," said Skeggs. "That ain't the way, not no more. We'll draw lots for 'er. 'Ighest number gets first ride—after me."

"I am afraid I cannot permit that," de Lacey told him quietly.

The Australian spat between his teeth. "Then you and me best get to it, Frenchy."

De Lacey nodded.

The men backed up.

"You pick the weapons," Skeggs said. The Australian was confident—unconcerned, even.

De Lacey smiled. "In that case, I make it interesting. I choose the weapon favorite to us both—the knife."

"Right," said Skeggs.

De Lacey removed his soft hat. He took his pistols from his sash and handed them to Reyes. He pulled a long, thin dagger from behind the sash and turned to face Skeggs.

"Right," the Australian repeated. "Knives it is." He laughed mockingly and pulled a pistol from his coat. "You stupid bloody fool."

De Lacey went cold. He stared death in the face. "I had not thought you were so clever," he said.

Skeggs laughed again and thumbed back the hammer, "So long, Frenchy."

Before Skeggs could pull the trigger, there was the slap of leather, and Dennis Whip's Colt was pointed at the Australian's temple.

"Fight fair, Skeggs," the slender gunman ordered. He smiled through his sparse beard.

Skeggs was enraged. "Why, you little . . ." Then he calmed, and a sly grin came over him. "Set me up, did you. Whip? That's all right. I'll take Frenchy 'ere either way. Then I'll see to you."

Skeggs lowered the revolver hammer and handed the weapon to Wabash. He threw away his hat and drew his double-edged knife with the brass knuckles.

Skeggs and de Lacey faced each other. Skeggs crouched; de Lacey rested on the bails of his feet, with his free hand high for balance—like the trained swordsman that he was. De Lacey knew that Skeggs was used to quick, decisive encounters. Many of Skegg's victories had come with just a few hard slashes—often at men who were unarmed.

The two men circled. Their feet scraped the dirt. Skeggs moved his knife point in and out, searching for an opening. De Lacey watched him, on guard. He found it curiously amusing to be fighting for the honor of a woman he intended to kill. The Australian didn't have much patience, and de Lacey knew he wouldn't wait long.

Skeggs feinted, feinted again, then dug quickly at de Lacey's face. The Frenchman skipped backward, parrying the blow with a *cling* of the blades.

They circled again. The Australian charged, slashing. De Lacey jumped back as the blade ripped through his buckskins, just missing his guts. When the Australian stopped, de Lacey lunged at him. Skegg's guard was too good to inflict serious damage, but de Lacey ripped his forearm with the knife point. The momentum of de Lacey's rush carried him past the Australian. He stopped quickly and turned, ready again.

Skeggs shook his wounded arm angrily. He charged again, directing a vicious jab at de Lacey's head. As the Frenchman ducked aside, Skeggs followed with a smash from the brass knuckles. De Lacey raised his arm. The knuckles bit to the bone, sending a jolt of pain through his body. Skeggs then directed a lunge to de Lacey's unguarded stomach. It almost worked. In his haste to escape Skeggs's blade, de Lacey tripped and fell. He caught himself on one hand, rolled away and came to his feet again, free hand held high.

Skeggs stopped for breath. De Lacey attacked. Skeggs got his guard up hurriedly, so de Lacey dropped his point and slashed the Australian across the thigh.

"Ow!" yelled Skeggs.

They faced each other again. Blood flowed from Skeggs's arm and thigh. His shaven head glistened with sweat. There was sweat in his eyes, and he wiped it away. De Lacey was businesslike, focused.

Skeggs gathered his strength and came at de Lacey again. He wanted to get this over with. The Frenchman had picked open ground, with room to move. He let Skeggs chase him, parrying the Australian's blows, tiring him out. At last Skeggs stopped. His chest heaved loudly; his face was red. He lowered his tired knife arm, and de Lacey ran in. The Australian tried to stab back in self-defense, but with a move quicker than the eye could follow, de Lacey flicked his blade past Skeggs's guard and drove it deep into his chest.

De Lacey turned. Skeggs was sinking to his knees. The Australian grabbed futilely at the long blade embedded in his chest. He sucked air for breath, but there was already a rattle in his throat. Blood stained the front of his dirty wool shirt. He looked up at his old companion de Lacey as if he couldn't understand what was happening to him. He fell over slowly, until his forehead rested on the ground. He remained on his knees. His hoarse gasps for air grew weaker and weaker, then he jerked and they ceased altogether.

De Lacey kicked the heavy body onto its back. Placing his foot on Skeggs's chest, he yanked his knife free. He wiped the knife blade clean with a handkerchief, then threw the handkerchief away.

He turned and faced the men, looking them in the eyes. "Does anyone else question my authority?"

No one answered. Some of the men looked at the ground.

De Lacey turned to Dennis Whip. "A timely piece of work. Mr. Whip. You have my gratitude. You are now my second in command." He paused, smiling. "But then, you knew that, didn't you?"

The gunman looked at his brother. Then he smiled back at de Lacey. "Let's say I suspicioned it."

Chapter 14

They left the promontory at dusk.

The Apaches had not been seen again after the brief clash amid the rocks, but Jake had waited to be certain they'd gone. Apaches didn't usually stay at the scene of a fight past sundown.

Jake's hangover still throbbed. He felt absolutely drained, but he had to keep going. He and Alison helped Hammond onto one of the two remaining horses. Jake had bandaged the boy's wound with some strips of flannel that he kept in his saddlebags. The rifle slug had lodged deep in the boy's abdomen, too deep for Jake to dig out. The bleeding was slight now, but Hammond was in considerable pain, though he tried not to show it. Beneath his four-day growth of whiskers, his youthful face was drawn and pale.

Alison feared for her brother. She could not keep a quaver from her voice as she said, "Hang on, Hammond. We'll get you to a doctor."

Hammond shook his head forcefully. "No. We're going on."

"Hammond, no treasure on earth is worth—"

"You'll never get this chance again, Allie. This ball inside me doesn't hurt much. I'll get it taken out in Santa Fe, after we get the treasure. Besides, if anything is going to happen to me, it'll happen long before we could get to a doctor. Right, Jake?"

Alison turned to Jake, who hesitated, then nodded. "That's right." Jake had seen wounds like this before, from Cerro Gordo to Diamond Bar, from the Yellowstone to the Platte, to the bayous of Texas and Louisiana. Some boys pulled through; most didn't. Jake didn't tell Hammond and Alison how gangrene smelled. He didn't tell them about the sickly yellow pus it produced. He didn't tell them how it rotted men alive from the inside.

The last light faded from the sky, and the desert was plunged into darkness. They started across the cactus-filled basin. Jake walked, leading Hammond's horse. The moon rose, and its light enabled them to climb back into the rock-covered hills. They inched along narrow, treacherous paths where a misstep could mean a broken leg, or worse.

They had to make up for lost time. If de Lacey was behind them, he would have heard the shots this morning. He'd be coming hard on their trail—or as hard as he could without water. Jake hoped there would be time to get to Dead Man's Canyon and get away again before the outlaws arrived.

At sunrise, they rested the horses and fed them. When they were ready to move on, Alison said, "You ride, Colonel. I'll walk for a while."

Jake looked at her through reddened eyes. "That's all right, I—"

"I said I'll walk. I'm not helpless, you know."

They got Hammond back on his horse, and Alison took its reins. Hammond had endured the jolting night ride better than Jake had expected. The boy's jaw was clenched tight against the pain. Beads of sweat rolled off his forehead. There was fear in his face.

They drank some water, then Jake adjusted the white mare's stirrups and hauled himself up. They set off. Alison walked easily, showing little sign of her fatigue. Despite the heat and the lack of food, Alison actually looked better than she had when she arrived in Tucson. The exercise seemed to have filled her out; her actions were less constrained, more natural. Her face powder and lip coloring were gone. The sunburn on her face was turning to tan, with only her cheeks still red, giving her a healthy look. Her blond hair was pinned loosely, a style that Jake found more becoming than the elaborate curls of before. Despite her worry over Hammond—or maybe because of it—her blue eyes sparkled with vitality.

Unlike Alison, Jake felt dull and incredibly tired. The powder burn on his face stung where sweat dripped into it. He cursed himself. He had made another mistake. He had fallen asleep and allowed the Apaches to get close. But that wasn't the worst part. If he hadn't been so proud, so eager to defend his life of lies, Hammond would be all right now. If he had just told the boy the truth, things would have been different. Hammond would never have jumped up on those rocks. He would never have been shot.

They camped that evening in a hollow. They propped Hammond against his saddle. With Jake's bowie knife, Alison cut up her spare linen blouse to make more bandages. Jake was apprehensive as he unwound the old wrapping. He took it off and let out his breath with relief. The wound looked fair, so far. There was some discoloration and a little seepage of blood. It smelled fresh, though; that was the important thing.

Alison knelt beside Jake, bathing her brother's feverish forehead and face with a wet cloth. "Maybe the worst is past," she said. "Maybe he'll be all right."

"Maybe," said Jake.

He washed the wound with water, then gently put on the new bandage. Hammond shuddered under his touch. "It hurts," he said.

Jake tried to buck up the boy's spirits as he tied the cloth. "Don't worry, son; you'll be fine. I've lived through worse than this. Why, I took nine bayonet wounds at the battle of Chapultapec."

Suddenly all of Hammond's pent-up fear came pouring out. "That's all right for you to say! You're Jake Moran. You're a hero. I'm not. I'm hurt and I'm scared, and I don't care who knows it."

Jake hung his head. He couldn't lie to the boy, not anymore. He must tell Hammond the truth. God, he could use a drink.

He put his hand on Hammond's shoulder. In a low voice, he said, "I'm no hero. All those things they say about me, I never done any of 'em. The men I killed; it was mostly by accident, or—"

"Accident!" Hammond struggled upright, wincing from the pain. He looked incredulous. "But—but that can't be. When you shot it out with the Coleman Gang, that was no . . ."

"The Coleman Gang was a bunch of half-baked horse thieves pulling their first job." Jake rose and looked into the fading light. "Me and my deputies followed them to an old farmhouse outside Leavenworth. We fired a volley, and they gave up. They was just scared kids. They wasn't killed in no gunfight. They was strung up by the fellows whose horses they stole."

Jake shifted on his feet. "Not long after that, a fellow from the *New York World Herald* come to Leavenworth to write the truth about wild and woolly Kansas. Did his research in saloons, mostly. Some of my deputies started telling this fellow tales, just to see what he'd fall for. He fell for a lot, and the result was that story about me wiping out the Coleman Gang. I was already known out here, but that story was the one that got me famous back east. When it went over big, the newspaper fellow wanted more stories about me, and the boys obliged him. I went along with it at first—the boys were just having a good time. I never dreamed anybody would take it serious. I never dreamed what it would do to my life."

"But Chief Spotted Deer," said Hammond. "What about the famous hand-to-hand combat, with your wrists tied together? You mean that was all . . . made up?"

Jake couldn't look the boy in the eye. "Far's I know, there never was no Chief Spotted Deer. If there was. I never met him."

"And Chapultapec? Was that made up, too?"

"No, that part's true—far as it goes. I was the first man into the castle, but only because it was certain death to go back. The Mexicans had wiped out my company, and their fire was concentrated down the hill, at our second line. It was safer to keep going forward. I was . . . I was trying to surrender when I got them bayonet wounds. Then the regiment came charging through behind me, and instead of being a coward, I was a hero for leading the way."

Jake turned away. He'd never told that to anyone. He couldn't bear to see the expression on the boy's face. "Chapultapec started it all. Because I was first man in, they made me an officer. Because I'd been an officer and a hero, they wanted me on the Frisco Vigilance Committee. Then, because I'd been a vigilante, they made me deputy marshal in Kansas. Because I'd done all them other things, they made me a colonel of cavalry and gave me a regiment when the war with the North started. Seems like one thing leads to another, like I don't have no control over it. I just want to be an ordinary man, but people won't let me."

The camp was silent. Hammond lay back on the saddle, staring at the night sky. Alison looked at Jake with her head cocked to one side. "I must confess. Colonel, I'm surprised. Not because you haven't done the things for which you are famous, but because you've admitted it. Why do you lie about your life? Why do you pretend to be something you're not?"

Jake shrugged. "Habit, I reckon. When you're a hero, people expect you to act a certain way. It's hard to stop.

After a while, you're not sure who you really are. It gets easier to go along with the lie than it would be to quit."

"So why tell us the truth?" she said.

"I don't know. It's important that you and—that you and Hammond know, somehow."

Jake heard Hammond sigh. Alison said. "If being a hero is repugnant to you, why didn't you go home after Mexico? Why come west?"

"Wasn't no place for me at home. Pa was leaving the farm to my older brother, Matt. Pa didn't want me around, anyway. He blamed me for my brother Ben's death."

Jake didn't know what else to say. He wished he could find some physical release for his torment. He could almost sense Alison feeling sorry for him, and he didn't want that. "We better get some sleep," he said gruffly.

Alison adjusted Hammond's blanket, and the three of them lay down. Jake couldn't sleep. He heard Hammond rustling, turning uncomfortably, and he knew that the boy couldn't sleep, either.

Above Jake, the stars shone like diamonds in a field of black velvet. He saw a shooting star cross the heavens, like his own star—briefly brilliant, soon vanished. He wished he had a drink. A drink to make his mind go blank. A drink to make him sleep. He looked over at his saddlebags, where his last bottle of Red Dog was packed. He rubbed his face with a scarred hand and then flexed his fingers nervously. Should he open the bottle?

He reached out his hand. Then he drew it back, licking his lips. He was trembling and shivering, but not from malaria. At last, he drifted into a troubled sleep.

He woke before dawn. Across from him, Alison was just rising. Jake looked away; he couldn't face her gaze. As the first gray light crept across the desert he drew on his boots and walked across the hollow to where Hammond lay propped on the saddle. Hammond looked curiously calm and composed. Yesterday's fear was gone from his boyish face. It had been replaced by a sort of peacefulness.

As Jake got close to Hammond, he stopped. He'd caught the smell. The smell of decay, of rot.

He forced himself to go on. He knelt slowly. The smell was stronger now. Alison smelled it, too, and she looked at Jake in alarm. Jake pulled down Hammond's blanket. With trembling fingers, he opened the boy's shirt.

Hammond's abdomen was swollen, and around the extremities it was turning purple. An evil-smelling, yellow-green pus was suppurating through his bandages.

Chapter 15

Hammond was remarkably calm. "I'm going to die, aren't I, Jake?"

Behind Jake, Alison sucked in her breath.

Jake forced himself to hold the boy's gaze. *No more lies.* "That's right, son. You're going to die."

Alison turned away.

Hammond said, "Come on, Sis, don't break down. I want to remember you like you've always been—mean and bossy." He laughed weakly at his joke.

Alison looked at Jake, her eyes distraught. "You're certain?"

Jake nodded.

Alison took a deep breath, steeling herself. She knelt beside Hammond and took his hand. "I'll stay with you, Hammond. I'll make you as—as comfortable as possible."

Hammond shook his head. His face was sweating; the wound must be giving him considerable pain. "No, Allie. You and Jake go. Leave me be."

"Hammond, I couldn't leave you now. I—"

"You have to. De Lacey could come over that ridge any minute. Stay, and he'll catch you."

"I don't care about that anymore," Alison said.

"You know what will happen if he gets you. Do you think I want that?"

Alison glanced at Jake. Jake's look told her the boy was speaking sense.

"Besides," said Hammond, "I want to be by myself."

Alison turned back, "Why? what's going to . . ."

Hammond looked to one side, where his revolvers lay.

Alison followed his gaze. She bit her lower lip. "Oh, Hammond."

"It's the best way, Allie. I'm going to die. I've known that since I was shot. I don't want it to be long and painful. I want to go out like a man. I want to prove myself."

"You have proved yourself," Jake said in a low voice. "More than once. Wasn't for you back in them rocks, we'd all be dead."

Hammond stared down at his stained bandages. He brushed the flies away mechanically. "All my life I've felt inadequate—helpless, somehow. I guess that's why I idolized a man like Colonel Jake Moran. But what you said last night got me thinking. I realized there's nothing wrong with me; there's nothing wrong with being scared. Heroes can be scared, too. I feel a lot better now. I can accept what's going to happen. It's the luck of the draw, as you would say, Jake."

Jake felt a tear start in his eye. He saw in Hammond's manner of dying the kind of courage he himself did not possess. He felt envious and ashamed.

Alison stroked Hammond's long straight hair back from his forehead. "I'm still going to stay, Hammond. For a while, at least. I don't even know where I'd go, if I did leave."

"Go?" said Hammond. "Go after the treasure, of course."

"I don't want the treasure now. There's no reason—"

"There's all the reason." Hammond told her. He tried to rise, and she had to hold him down lest he hurt himself. "Do you think we came all this way just for you to turn back? Was my getting shot for nothing? What will you do without money? Prostitution is the only occupation I've heard of for women in this part of the country, and you're hardly suited for that."

Alison looked at him bleakly.

"You're too close to give up now, Allie. Prove we can do it. Prove it for Father's sake. Prove it for me." He gripped her hand. "I want you to promise me you'll find that treasure—you and Jake." He looked from one to the other. "Please, it—it means a lot to me."

Alison's eyes glistened. Softly she said, "All right, Hammond. I promise."

Jake nodded solemnly.

"Good," said Hammond. He shifted a bit, wincing with pain. "Now get out of here before you start me crying." He turned his head away from them.

Jake rose to his feet. So did Alison. They glanced at each other. Alison looked lost. She was obviously blaming herself for what had happened, and it wasn't her fault. Jake took her arm gently and led her away. "Come on."

Alison fed and watered the horses. Jake saddled them. It didn't take long. They walked back to Hammond. "We're ready," said Jake.

Alison closed her eyes as if she was praying.

Hammond propped himself more comfortably on the saddle. The putrid smell of the gangrene seemed to have grown stronger. Jake hesitated, then placed Hammond's revolver belt within reach.

Hammond pulled one of the weapons from its holster. "Take this. You might need it."

"Save it," Jake said quietly, kneeling so that Alison could not hear. "In case the first one misfires. Put the barrel in your mouth. Man shoots himself in the temple, he sometimes lives for days."

Hammond swallowed, thinking of what was to come. Then he nodded.

Jake rose. He looked down, sneering inwardly at himself. He was so good at helping people die. Why couldn't he have been as good at helping the boy stay alive?

Then he remembered something. He walked to his horse. From his saddlebag he took his last bottle of Red Dog. He returned and handed the bottle to Hammond. "I reckon your sister won't mind."

Alison sniffed and brushed back a tear, forcing herself to smile. "Just this once," she said.

Hammond rummaged in his possessions and pulled out a book. The stiff paper cover showed a fierce-looking man, long-haired and clad in fringed buckskins. The man was hatless, his empty pistol lay at his feet, and he was wielding his rifle as a club. Beside him stood a woman wearing a buckskin dress and a wide bandana, holding her rifle in the same position. Circled around them was a horde of painted savages with lances and shields and tufts of feathers in their hair. The book's title was *Jake Moran Meets Hurricane Nell.*

"I bought this before we left Baltimore," Hammond explained apologetically. "I might as well see how it comes out."

Jake said nothing.

Hammond turned to his sister. "Well . . ."

Alison fell to her knees and threw her arms around the boy, crying, "Oh, Hammond." He clasped her.

Jake turned away. He felt embarrassed to watch, as if he were intruding upon their privacy. Beneath Alison's cool exterior was a wellspring of emotion. She looked exceedingly vulnerable right now, and Jake felt sorry for her.

At last Hammond gently pushed his sister away. "Good-bye, Allie."

"Good-bye, Hammond," she said, but she made no effort to rise. Hammond looked at Jake, who took Alison's elbow and helped her to her feet. Her hands left her brother's reluctantly.

Jake knelt beside Hammond. He offered his hand. The boy took it. "So long, Hammond," Jake said.

"So long, Jake. Take care of Allie."

"I will."

"I know you will," Hammond said.

Jake stood. He wondered why Hammond still trusted him. after what he'd done to the boy. This was the human wreckage that Jake's reputation left in its wake.

Hammond had tried to be like Jake Moran—or what he imagined Jake Moran to be—and this was how he'd paid for it.

Hammond made a big show of opening the book and preparing to read. He shook the bottle of Red Dog, watching it foam, then uncorked it.

Jake and Alison walked to their horses. Alison moved stiffly, keeping her eyes on her horse, lest she break down. Her face was wet, her eyes red. Her mouth was uncertain, though she tried to hold it firm.

They led the horses from the hollow. Jake helped Alison onto the white mare, then he mounted Hammond's chestnut gelding. They looked back. Hammond was watching them. He raised his hand in farewell.

Jake raised his in return. Alison looked away, crying. They turned their horses and rode off toward Dead Man's Canyon. The morning sun threw their shadows far across the hills. They rode in silence. There was nothing to say.

It was several hours before they heard the pistol shot.

Chapter 16

Jake reckoned it was time to leave the mountains. He and Alison followed a winding canyon back to the valley. covering their tracks as best they could. They reached the valley and started across. Jake figured they must be a good seventy miles southwest of Tucson. He had been through this country twice before, in the Fifties. The Mexican border was not far from here.

Just after noon, Jake led Alison to a lonely eminence in the middle of the valley. They climbed it and dismounted below some tall boulders. Here they had a broad view of the valley, which from this height seemed perfectly flat. In reality, it was creased by undulations and dry washes and choked with brush so that you could hide a thousand men out there without them being seen.

Jake unsaddled the horses and turned them loose for what little grazing they could find. He took his Yankee field glasses from their leather case and lay between the rocks, where his outline did not show against the horizon. With the glasses, he watched their back trail. He watched it for a long time, chewing the end of his mustache. Below him, Alison stared into the distance. She had taken off her straw hat. She had not spoken since they'd left Hammond. She was fighting her emotions, trying not to show them, as she'd probably been taught at that seminary.

When Jake was satisfied there was no one behind them, he turned slowly, searching the horizon in all directions. At last he lowered the field glasses and walked back down the hill to Alison. "No sign of de Lacey," he said. "Either we threw him off our trail or the loss of water's hurting him bad. Maybe some of his horses have died. Maybe he's even turned back."

Jake took a long drink from his canteen. "He didn't run into the Apaches, or we'd have heard shooting. I reckon the Indians have gone to hit their target—God help whoever that is. No telling what route they'll use to return to the Dragoon Mountains. Just pray it don't come near us."

Alison said nothing. She was trembling all over.

Jake motioned to where a long ridge projected into the valley, about ten miles ahead of them. Erosion had worn the foot of this ridge into three rocky towers of roughly the same size. Jake had seen the towers while they were climbing the eminence, but Alison seemed not to have noticed.

"There's your three buttes," Jake said.

Alison made no response. Tears were running out of her eyes and down her cheeks.

Jake set the field glasses on a rock. He reached out to Alison. He turned her and drew her to him. She came willingly. She buried her head in his shoulder and broke down crying. Jake smoothed her back, trying not to think about the soft, womanly feel of her body pressed against his, trying to ignore the heady woman smell. He looked across the sun-baked valley, letting Alison sob out her grief.

"He doesn't even have a cross over him," she murmured at last. "He doesn't even have a *grave*. He's just lying out there, for the animals to . . ." Her voice broke off. Her face was filled with self-hate, as if she felt that she had let her brother down.

Jake smoothed her blond hair. He spoke in a low voice. "That sort of thing don't make no difference, not in the long run. It's how a man lived his life that counts."

She was blaming herself for Hammond's death, and it was Jake's fault. He tilted her chin and looked in her eyes. "Hammond was a man, Alison, a good man. As good as they come. That's how you should remember him. You let that be some comfort to you."

Alison backed away, wiping her nose and cheeks, brushing wetness from the corner of her eye. "I never should have let him come."

"Stop being so hard on yourself. Hammond was old enough to make his own decisions. You couldn't have stopped him."

Alison sniffed again. She smiled at some memory of her brother. "I suppose you're right. Ever since he was a little boy, Hammond was determined to have a 'Great Adventure' in the West. If he hadn't come with me, he'd have come on his own."

"Boys are mostly the same at that age," Jake said. He remembered his brother Ben; he remembered Ben's laughing self-confidence. "Growing up can be cruel."

Alison turned away. She looked down at her suntanned hands. "I feel lost without Hammond—much as you must have felt after losing your brother. For most of our lives. Hammond and I had no one but ourselves."

"What about your father?"

"Our father lived only to drink. He was a wonderful man when sober, but when he was drinking he became a monster. I can remember walking the streets, dragging Hammond with me, searching the saloons for Father so we'd have money to buy food—like something from a Dickens novel. I remember Father screaming in the dead of night, fighting the horrors that only he could see. I remember him lying in bed for days afterward, lapping milk like a weak kitten. I used to believe his condition was brought on by Mother's death and the loss of his fortune. Then I read his letter, and I learned the real reason."

Alison drew a long sigh. There was a tremor in her voice again. "It's funny. My greatest fear for Hammond was never that he would get himself hurt. It was always that he would become a drunkard, like Father. Now I'd almost rather he'd been a drunk. At least he'd be alive."

"No, you don't," said Jake softly. "You don't wish nothing of the kind."

Alison cried again, and Jake held her. Finally, he said, "We better get going."

Jake watered the horses and fed them some of the dwindling corn supply. Then he saddled them. When he and Alison had mounted, he took out his field glasses once again and scanned the horizon. Alison watched him, contemplating.

Jake put the field glasses away, and the horses picked a path down from the eminence. "Do none of these stories about you have a basis in fact?" Alison asked.

Ahead of her, Jake shifted in his saddle, uncomfortable with the question. "Some of 'em happened. They got exaggerated is all."

"For instance?"

Jake squirmed a bit. "Well . . . for instance, once I was ridin' mail on the Feather River, in California, when I got jumped by a bunch of de Lacey's men. There was a scrap, and I rode off. They tried to catch me, but they couldn't. During the chase, one of 'em fell off his horse, broke his neck, and got killed. The story got to be that I shot that fella to death. Folks wouldn't believe anything else—they still won't. I think even de Lacey believes it."

"Just to have outridden them must have been a considerable feat," Alison said. She, who had been Jake's accuser, was now defending him. "And despite what you say about yourself, it took a deal of courage to confront Mr. de Lacey and his gang the other night. One man against ten."

Jake snorted. "Believe me, lady, if there was another way. I'd have tried it."

After a moment, Alison said, "What would you have done if they had not started to torture Hammond?"

Jake shrugged. "I had some plan about coming into camp at night and sneaking you two off. Probably it wouldn't have worked. Smart thing would have been to sneak up on de Lacey's men one by one on the trail and shoot them in the back."

"So why didn't you do that?"

"Ain't smart, I reckon. That, or I ain't got the guts."

They kept the three buttes ahead of them. Sometimes it didn't seem the buttes were drawing closer at all; other times it seemed they'd jumped a whole piece forward at once. It was late in the afternoon when Jake and Alison rounded the crumbling base of the westernmost butte and entered Dead Man's Canyon.

The canyon was narrow at first, but it widened considerably after taking a dogleg right. The bottom was bone-dry this August. Jake and Alison rode in cathedral shadows. It was another world in there; the high canyon walls shut off the life of the desert outside. Birds called; the breeze rustled the sycamores and scrub oaks and desert willow. Brush grew thick along the banks and on what were islands when the water was running. Juniper pine and cedars could be seen higher up. Far above them, a hawk glided across the narrow opening of sky.

"Look," said Alison, pointing.

There was something painted on the rocks across the canyon. Large images in red and white. Jake and Alison nudged their horses closer.

The rock here ran sheer for about fifty yards. The images, which about three feet tall, had been painted at eye level to a standing man. Around the borders of the mural were abstract geometrical designs, whorls and crosses. Inside were drawings of men. These men wore large headdresses and necklaces, earrings and sashes, and they carried shields. All were shown with arrows in their backs. A few were standing, but most lay horizontally, with their big-eyed, square heads separated from their bodies. The edges of the heads were jagged, as if they had been cut off.

A chill gripped Jake's spine. He shifted uneasily in the saddle.

"What does it mean?" Alison asked.

"Don't know," said Jake. "A warning, maybe."

Alison touched one of the drawings gingerly. She looked at her fingers; the paint had not rubbed off. "These figures resemble the Hokokam art I was shown when I was researching my pretense of being an archeologist. These are different from anything I saw, though, especially in their depiction of violence."

Jake's throat had gone unnaturally dry. "This place might have been called Dead Man's Canyon a lot longer than you think."

"Mr. de Lacey says it is haunted."

Jake twisted in the saddle, looking around. "Don't much believe in ghosts myself."

"Nor do I. All the same, I have an eerie feeling—like we're being watched."

Jake had the same feeling, but he didn't want to admit it to Alison. "Come on," he said.

The canyon took another sharp turn. It was now nearly a half-mile wide. Ahead, a tall spire of rock pointed heavenward from the sand, completely cut off from the canyon walls.

"There's the Needle," Alison said. "Father's map is correct so far."

Another quarter hour's riding brought them to the rise on which the spring was located. The water's location stood out clearly in a splash of green. Something else stood out as well—dun-colored adobe.

"Somebody's built a house up there," said Jake. He studied the structure through his field glasses. "It's deserted. We can go on. "

They were approaching the rise when Alison's mare shied from something in its path. Alison looked down and gave a cry.

A human skull was grinning at her through the weeds.

There was a large hole in the skull's side. Suddenly a dark snake, fully eight feet long, slithered through the hole and vanished in the undergrowth. Alison's horse reared with fright. Jake caught her reins, steadying it.

Alison was unnerved. "Was that a rattlesnake?"

"Bullsnake," said Jake. "He won't hurt you." Jake was uneasy, too, and he didn't know why. He'd seen skulls and snakes before.

They rode on. Around them they saw more skulls, and bones. The bones were decayed and brittle and bleached a yellowish white from age and the sun. They were no longer in human form. They had been scattered across a wide expanse of the canyon floor, both by the forces of nature and by animals who'd dragged them away.

"This is where the soldiers were shot," said Alison. She looked around, curbing her nervous horse, trying to visualize that night of horror twenty-nine years before.

Jake got down and poked around. He found some bridle bits, a haversack clasp. "Apaches took the soldiers' weapons and most of the metal," he said. "What they couldn't use themselves, they must have melted and sold back to the Mexicans."

Something caught his eye, and he pried it from the sand. It was an officer's braided brass epaulette, green with tarnish. He scraped the dirt off it. It had belonged to a major, he guessed from the star and wreath engraved on the surface. Jake held it for a moment, wondering about the man who had worn it, wondering whose career had ended in these rank weeds. Then he tossed it away.

He mounted, and they rode up the rise to the spring. The adobe house was set back from the edge of the rise, shaded by cottonwood trees. It was in ruins; two of its sides and all of the roof save a beam had fallen in. To the rear was a crumbled corral and some scattered lumber that might have once been sheds.

"A ranch?" said Alison.

Jake nodded. "Must have been deserted a good twenty years ago. Hasn't been ranches in this part of the country since the Forties, on account of the Apaches." He looked around. "Reckon Apaches got this bunch, too."

"Apaches or ghosts," said Alison uneasily.

"We'll camp here. It's too late to look for the treasure today."

Jake unsaddled the horses, who made for the spring. Above them, water, brought forth by enormous pressure inside the earth, trickled out of the rock wall. It ran down the mossy rock into a small pool, which overflowed into another, larger pool.

Jake walked around the spring. He saw animal tracks, but no sign of Indians. That was funny. This pool must be the only water for fifty miles, this time of year. The absence of tracks didn't mean that much, though. A man could approach the spring by the talus of the rock walls and never leave a sign of his passing. Jake lay beside the larger pool and scooped water into his mouth. It was cold, with a strong mineral taste. The feel of the soft grass against his body was delicious.

Nearby, Alison splashed water on her face, washing away the trail dirt. She poured more on her neck, obviously luxuriating in its cooling effect.

Twilight came on. Frogs started croaking by the spring. Jake fed and hobbled the horses. "We'll sleep in the house. It'll shelter us from the wind, at least."

The house was a mess of lumber and weeds and crumbled adobe blocks. There was a rusted portable stove, a battered bucket, assorted odds and ends. They ate stewed jerky and pan-fried bread. Jake made coffee. When they were done, he walked to the edge of the rise and took a last look around with his field glasses.

He came back and, after scraping an area free of rubble and spiders, he spread the blankets—his in one corner, Alison's in another. He felt ill at ease alone here with her, sleeping within feet of her. He tried not to think of her as a woman; he tried not to think of her as desirable. She had saved his life, and, according to what honor he had, he was bound to see her to Santa Fe—if they lived that long.

They stood looking awkwardly at each other. "Well," said Alison at last, "tomorrow we go for the treasure."

"Yeah," said Jake, "tomorrow." Despite the map's accuracy so far, Jake still didn't believe there was treasure here. Apache arrows and thirty years of whiskey played tricks on a man's memory. "Better get some sleep," he said. He touched his hat. "Good night, Miss Shaw." Then he grinned. "Alison."

"Good night, Jake."

They rolled themselves in their blankets. They slept undisturbed.

Chapter 17

Jake's malaria struck the next morning as they were saddling the horses.

Alison led Jake back to the ruined adobe house. He was suffering badly from the chills, and she wrapped him in blankets to warm him.

"Thanks," he said between clenched teeth.

After the chills came fever. Jake's forehead was burning. He tossed in semi-delirium. Alison shifted him so that he was in the shade. She bathed his unshaven face with cool water, then held the canteen to his lips. Her hands trembled when she touched him, and she could not make them stop.

At last the fever began to subside. Jake's breathing became more regular. His blue flannel shirt was soaked through with sweat. Alison opened his saddlebags to get his dry red shirt, thinking to make him more comfortable. As she pulled the shirt out, something dropped from the saddlebag—a sepia-tinted daguerreotype.

Alison picked up the daguerreotype. It showed an attractive girl, light-complexioned, in her late teens or early twenties. The girl was wearing a fireman's uniform and fancy suspenders, and a big helmet with the number six on the crest.

Alison saw Jake watching her. She said. "Your wife, I suppose? Or is it one of your paramours?" She was surprised at the bitterness in her voice.

Jake struggled up on one elbow. His fever-wracked eyes burned with anger. "She ain't my wife, and she ain't no paramour, or whatever the hell you called her."

Alison's look demanded further explanation.

Jake hesitated. Reluctantly, he went on. "Her name's Evelyn Malloy. When she was five I pulled her out of a burning building in San Francisco. Her family was all killed in the fire, and I sort of became her godfather. Most of whatever money I've made over the years I've sent to her, for her education and such. Every year she has her picture taken in my old volunteer fireman's helmet and sends it to me. She's getting married next spring to a real nice fellow, from one of the best families in San Francisco. I'm just hoping I can be there to see it."

He sank back. That little bit of exertion had tired him. Alison gave him some water from the canteen. "I— I'm sorry," she said.

She looked at the ugly burn scars on Jake's hands and arms. "Then you really *are* a hero," she said.

"Who, me?" Jake shook his head. "Any man in Big Six would have done the same. I just happened to be closest to the room where she was trapped. It happened quick; it's nothing to talk about." He looked at his scarred hands ruefully. "A friend of mine slipped a wet hood over my head as I went in, but I didn't have no gloves."

Alison could not get over her surprise—though in a way she was not surprised at all. "Why isn't this story a part of your legend?"

Jake laughed weakly. "Reckon folks want to hear about me shooting people, not saving their lives."

Soon after, he fell into a deep sleep. Alison didn't wake him. Time was important, but it was also essential that Jake regain strength. It was after noon when they finished saddling the horses and started up the canyon to find the treasure.

Jake felt weak, but otherwise all right. Alison looked utterly confident. He hoped her confidence was justified, for both their sakes.

Tom Shaw's map had located the rock window about two-and-a-half miles from the spring. It was hard to judge distance in the twisting canyon, and it must have been even harder for Shaw, running from the Apaches. Jake and Alison rounded bend after bend, and the canyon narrowed, but they saw no window. They'd gone a good three miles by Jake's reckoning when Alison, who was riding ahead, motioned him forward.

"Jake," she said in a quiet voice.

He came up to her. High above them, to the right, the forces of nature had formed an almost perfectly circular opening in the rock—a window—beyond which could be seen the bright blue of the sky.

Jake felt a tightness in the pit of his stomach. Could there be something to this treasure story?

"The marker should be somewhere along here," Alison said. "It's supposed to look like a pyramid."

153

They dismounted, searching up and down both sides of the canyon, pushing aside the thick brush. Things had changed here in twenty-nine years. They were in the sun, and it was hot work.

Jake kicked his way through another stand of flowering yellow rabbitbush. He found nothing. He stopped to catch his breath. Sweat was pouring off him, and he drank some water. He was looking at a small pile of flat rocks next to him. Then his heart stopped beating for a second as he realized it was a *pile* of rocks. It had been put there by human hands. It was, in fact, in somewhat the shape of a pyramid.

"Good God," he said softly. He'd almost missed it—he'd been looking for something larger. Then he raised his voice. "Alison! This way!"

Alison hurried over, leaving her horse. As she looked at the marker, Jake turned toward the window in the rock. "It's here," he said. "The treasure's really here."

Alison was breathing hard, her eyes alight. She said, "Now we align this marker with the window and count a hundred seventeen steps up. We'll come to a rock ledge. Move left along the ledge until we find a boulder with a cross on it. The treasure is in a large chamber of the cave behind that boulder."

They tied the horses, then clambered up the rocks with Jake in the lead, counting their steps. Jake was thinking about mules. At the time, it hadn't bothered him when they'd lost their mules to the Apaches. He hated mules, and he'd never believed they'd need them. Now he wished they had those mules. He wished they had them bad.

At a hundred paces, they began looking hard for the ledge. "There it is," said Jake, "just above us."

The ledge was a natural walkway along the surface of the rock wall. Jake and Alison followed it around a sharp bend in the canyon, moving carefully, testing footholds.

Around the bend they stopped. Their way was blocked by a fall of boulders. On the face of one of these boulders had been carved a crude cross.

Jake and Alison looked at each other, excitement rising in their breasts.

Jake squatted and peered behind the boulder. "Looks like a small opening back there. Can't see it good."

He stood. His legs trembled from the heat and the malaria. He raised his eyebrows. "Here goes." He put his shoulder to the boulder, grimacing from the effort. Alison threw her weight alongside his.

The boulder gave. They strained. The boulder rocked sideways. They let it roll back. "Again," gasped Jake. They heaved, and the boulder gave some more. They let it roll back again.

They were both breathing heavily. They looked at each other, their features animated by nothing more than a sheer lust for gold. "This one'll do it," Jake said.

They put their shoulders to the rock. They groaned, their faces contorted. The boulder rocked forward. It teetered onto its fulcrum. Then it fell over with a crash and bounced down the hill, smashing into some more rocks with a noise that echoed up and down the canyon.

The boulder had uncovered a small cave. Alison got on her knees and looked inside. "Wait," said Jake. "This is the kind of place rattlers like."

Jake cast around and began gathering brush for a primitive torch. "Use this," said Alison. From her boot she produced a wax candle. "I brought these all the way from Baltimore. I figured since the treasure was in a cave, we'd need them."

"Smart girl," said Jake. He lit the candle with a sulphur match. His head felt light; he was clumsy in his haste.

He got on his knees and shoved the candle into the cave. It was greeted by no warning rattle. He drew one of his four revolvers and wriggled through the opening. Alison followed close behind.

Jake crawled through the damp cave on one hand with the smoking candle thrust before him. The rock walls cast a thousand shadows in the flickering light. He coughed from the acrid smoke. Spider webs brushed his face and got in his mouth. Hundreds of black beetles swarmed over him, trying to get out of his way. He kept his finger on the trigger guard of the revolver.

Suddenly the cave opened onto a large chamber. Jake went weak inside, and he forgot all about rattlesnakes. Here was the treasure.

He paused by the opening. His heart was pounding with anticipation; his throat was dry. Alison came up beside him, and he could feel her excitement.

They moved inside. Jake held up the candle, and the two of them looked around in amazement.

The chamber was empty.

Chapter 18

Jake and Alison sagged, disbelieving. In the guttering candlelight they stared at the opposite wall of the chamber.

"The treasure's gone," said Alison.

"Somebody beat us to it," Jake said.

They sank onto the slimy rock floor. They felt listless, devoid of energy and purpose, as if they could just stay here forever, staring at that wall.

"I never expected this," Alison said numbly. "All that work, all that sorrow. It was all for nothing."

Jake had to laugh. He didn't know which was funnier— the monstrous joke that had been played on them or the expression on Alison's face. Alison looked at him for a moment, and then she laughed, too. They laughed together. Their laughter was self-mocking at first, but it grew harder and harder, until they were roaring, holding their sides, with tears running down their cheeks. Something had come over them; they couldn't stop. It was a release of all their disappointments, all their thwarted expectations. They laughed until they were red in the face and could laugh no more, their laughter echoing off the jagged rock walls of the chamber.

Afterward, they sat side by side, silently catching their breath. They sat for a long time. The candlelight made Alison's face radiant gold in the darkness, like a painting by an Old Master.

"I wonder who found it," she said at last.

"Well, it wasn't de Lacey," said Jake. "No human's been in this cave for years. My guess is Apaches removed the treasure right after they jumped your father's party."

Alison turned. "I thought Indians had no use for gold."

"Indians ain't stupid. They know they can use gold to buy weapons. Probably there's bits of that treasure cached from the Sierra Madres to the Guadalupes, still being used to buy guns to murder settlers."

They grew silent again. Jake looked over at Alison. With a jolt, he realized that he liked her. He liked her very much. She was staring at him. Her head was cocked; she was studying him with a frankness that he found disconcerting.

"It's getting late," he mumbled, rising. "We'd best get back."

They crawled back through the passage and out into the open air. The heat outside seemed even more torrid after the chilly cave. The late-afternoon sky had become brassy, but it was extremely bright after the candlelit darkness.

"We'll have to stay another night at the spring," Jake said. "We'd never get out of this canyon before dark. Besides, a storm's coming."

They made their way along the rock ledge and down the side of the canyon. It seemed to take much longer to go down the hill than it had to come up. Jake untied the horses and helped Alison mount. They paused for a last look up at the rock window, for a last thought about what might have been. Then they started back down the canyon.

They let the horses set their own pace. "What will you do now?" Alison asked Jake.

"Get you to Santa Fe, if I can. After that, who knows? Try for California, I reckon. What about you?"

Alison managed to look hopeful. "I have no money and no family, now that Hammond . . ." She paused, then went on. "Perhaps I can find a position as a governess in Santa Fe, or as a teacher. If I were a man, I could mine for gold, or drive a team, or get a job in a store. But I am a woman. I can be a governess, or I can teach, or . . . . You heard Hammond describe the alternative."

She turned away, tight-lipped.

The sun was almost down when they reached the roofless adobe. Jake tended the horses, then fixed supper. Neither of them was hungry. They caught themselves looking at each other, and they turned away awkwardly. Attempts at conversation died off. Their voices took on an unnatural huskiness; their words caught in their throats. The heat seemed more oppressive than ever.

A puff of wind blew, rustling the loose strands of Alison's hair. The wind grew stronger. The sky turned an opaque gold from the sand that the coming storm carried with it. The air had the thick smell of dust.

Jake and Alison crossed the cabin and looked over the crumbled wall. The wind blew stiffly now. Swollen purple thunderheads welled up in the distance, visible against the lowering dark. They heard the rumble of thunder. They saw lightning's flickering glow.

The wind strengthened and strengthened yet again. It howled around the trees and the rocks and the ruined adobe. Jake and Alison moved closer to the wall. Her golden hair struggled against its pins. His hat brim blew back, and he squinted against the stinging particles of dust that lashed his face.

It was dark now. Around the cabin, the invisible trees groaned as they bent in the wind, and Jake was afraid that one would come crashing over onto them. Suddenly a terrific bolt of lightning struck the ground nearby. Jake and Alison jumped closer to each other as thunder boomed around them and down the canyon.

The lightning's crack had snapped Jake's body like a whip. His hair stood on end, and he could feel the electricity rippling through him. His fingertips tingled. He was scared.

Lightning crashed again, lightning up Alison's terrified face. They were helpless. For all their struggle against their fellow men, their fate was a whim of nature. The echoes of the last thunder had not died away when the biggest bolt of lightning yet struck with a nerve-jarring crash. Jake and Alison moved closer again. Their shoulders were touching.

Jake trembled, his mouth dry. He felt Alison trembling, too. It was pitch dark. Another flash of lightning, and he saw her looking up at him. He saw her chest rising and falling as the thunder cannoned.

Jake reached out his hand. He shook her hair loose from its pins. It fell in cascades around her shoulders, then it was snapped away by the wind. He caught the hair in his hands. He ran his fingers through it gently. She did not stop him.

His heart was pounding; his head spun. Lightning flashed again, and he saw it reflected in the eyes that looked into his. He did not hear the thunder anymore. He ran his fingers down Alison's neck and along the tops of her shoulders. She moved under his touch. He let his hands come to rest on her waist. He drew her to him. He felt her arms go around him as he bent to kiss her. The taste of her lips was intoxicating; her body was soft and warm and yielding against his. He never wanted this moment to end.

As lightning flashed, and thunder pealed, and the wind blew down the canyon, Jake and Alison became lovers.

Chapter 19

Jake could not sleep. He sat up. It was the middle of the night. From his saddlebag, he got the makings of a *cigarillo* and lit it. The storm had passed without rain. The canyon seemed extraordinarily quiet now. The air was cooler, refreshing.

Jake dragged deeply on the *cigarillo*. He'd taken advantage of Alison. She had been put into his care, and he had seduced her. He had assumed a trust—if only self-imposed—and he had violated it.

Suddenly he wondered—was this the real reason Hammond had wanted him and Alison to go on? Had Hammond pictured the two of them coming together this way? Had the boy seen an attraction between them that they themselves had failed to notice? If so, he had made a mistake.

Beside him, Alison opened her eyes, awakened perhaps by the rank smell of the Mexican tobacco. Stretching, she rolled onto her side and looked at Jake's tall form silhouetted against the stars. Then she came onto her knees beside him, touching his arm. "You're sorry. Why?"

He did not look at her. When he spoke, he bit off the words, as if it hurt to say them. "I've behaved dishonorably toward you, Alison. You have my apologies."

Alison slid close to him. "No, Jake. You did nothing of the kind. We both wanted it. It was—it was lovely." Jake felt the warm flesh of her body against him. He felt her soft breasts, her nipples. It took all his self-control not to turn and throw himself on her. He swallowed. "I'm going to do the right thing by you, Alison, even though it may not seem that way to you now. When we get to Santa Fe, I'm going to leave you. Best to break this off before it goes any further."

Alison backed away, stunned. "But Jake, why?"

"Because you and me would never work. You're probably dreaming about taking me back east, about settling down in some city and showing me off to your society friends. Don't you see? I wouldn't be happy back there. I wouldn't fit in."

"I could be happy in California, Jake. I could be happy wherever you are."

"You think that now, but you'd change your mind. It's a rough life on the frontier. A lady like you who's been to seminary school and all just wouldn't—"

"Oh, Jake, I've never been to a seminary."

He looked at her, surprised. She continued, "I've hardly any formal education at all. I had to leave school to take care of Hammond and Father. Most of what I've learned has come from reading books and from watching others. I don't have any society friends. When I was a child, Father invested all his money in canal stocks, and when the railroads made canals obsolete, he lost every cent. By the time he died, we were living in a run-down boardinghouse near the docks."

She looked down. "These—these high-bred airs of mine are a defense, I suppose. I've found that if you act as if you *are* someone, people will treat you that way. I've acted like the person I thought I wanted to be, not like the person I am. I suppose we're alike in that respect."

Jake could hardly believe what he was hearing, but he had made up his mind. "That don't change a thing. There's too much hardship out here for a city woman. And danger, too—especially with me."

"What do you think I've been through this last week?" Alison cried. "If this isn't hardship and danger, I'd like to see what is."

"We're talking about a lifetime, not weeks," Jake snapped. She was in love with him, and that was the last thing that could be allowed to happen. There was one thing he hadn't wanted to bring up, but in a burst of self-anger he whirled on her. "Damn it, Alison, it's my fault Hammond is dead, and we both know it. It would always come between us."

"Jake, there was nothing you could have done to—"

"I could have told him the truth," Jake said. "I could have put some sense in his head instead of filling it with lies."

Alison grew quiet. She looked away. Then she said calmly, "Is your decision final?"

"It has to be."

He turned to her. Her naked body was a white blur in the dark; he tried not to look at it. He wanted to touch her, to comfort her, but he was afraid of what would happen. He hated this, but he had to do what was right.

He spoke in a low voice. "Believe me, Alison, I'm not the man for you. I'm not good enough for you. You'll thank me for this someday—when you've got that husband and babies."

He turned away and rolled another *cigarillo*. He was surprised that he did not want a drink. He realized that he had not wanted a drink in some while. At least some good had come of this, he thought bitterly.

Alison fell back on the blanket. She turned on her side so Jake wouldn't see her crying. After a while, she fell into a restless sleep.

* * *

She awakened to an incredibly loud bang not ten feet away. She jumped up, terrified, then got down again.

Jake was dressed, tucked against the ruined adobe wall, looking out at something. Smoke drifted from the barrel of the carbine. It was dawn.

Alison slipped on her clothes, keeping low. She joined Jake by the wall and glanced around the edge of the broken adobe.

The big outlaw named Wabash lay dead on his back no more than twenty feet away. One of his hands held a pistol; in the other was a string of canteens. Jake wasn't looking at Wabash, though. He was looking across the canyon, where a white flag fluttered from the rocks.

Chapter 20

Still waving the white handkerchief, Edouard de Lacey made his way down the rocks to the bottom of the canyon. With him was a man with silver conchos on his hat—Dennis Whip. The rest of the gang must be hidden in the rocks and brush. There was no sign of their horses.

"Colonel Moran! A word, if you please!" called the Frenchman. "There will be no violence toward your person—you have my promise. We are unarmed."

De Lacey's voice echoed down the canyon. Inside the ruined adobe, Jake and Alison watched. Jake thought the Frenchman's jauntiness looked forced. "Why's he want to talk?" Jake said. "He's got no intent of letting us leave here alive. Why don't he just come after us?"

"Will you meet with him?" said Alison.

"Can't see no harm in it. He's got us in a bad spot, real bad. It won't hurt to hear what he's got to say. Buy us some time, if nothing else."

Jake rose to his full height. He loosened his four revolvers in their holsters. He hefted the carbine and stepped across the crumbling adobe wall.

"You call that 'unarmed?' " Alison said.

Jake grinned. "You're the one always telling me I ain't no gentleman."

Alison gathered her Dragoon colt.

"No, you stay here," Jake said.

"The devil I will. You're not leaving me out of this."

Jake swore. There was no arguing with her. "All right, come on. But be careful."

They came slowly down from the house. Beyond the canyon rim the sun was just rising, probably the last sunrise they would ever see. Jake moved cautiously, scanning the canyon for movement, for the glint of a rifle barrel. If the outlaws were going to try something, they wouldn't do it at this range. They'd wait till he and Alison got to the bottom.

Jake was still shaking from the encounter with Wabash. That had been close—the big outlaw might have killed them both if it hadn't been for his noisy approach and Jake's inability to sleep. The horses, in the contrary way of horses, had raised no alarm, and Wabash had apparently failed to notice them in the dim light. Jake had waited till Wabash was right next to the house before challenging him. Wabash had acted surprised, and Jake had made a dead shot before the outlaw could raise his pistol. Maybe Wabash hadn't been looking for him and Alison on the rise, Jake thought; maybe he'd been looking for something else.

De Lacey and Whip were waiting in the shade of some sycamores. As he drew closer, Jake knew the reason Wabash had been on the rise. He knew the reason for this meeting. And his heart jumped, because it meant that he and Alison had a chance.

De Lacey and Whip were beat. Their lips were cracked, their eyes bright with the madness of thirst. De Lacey was barely recognizable. His buckskins were stained and torn; his red sash had taken on the color of dust. His once-elegant mustache was tangled and greasy; the imperial was nearly invisible against the heavy growth of his whiskers.

They must be desperate for water. Jake's move to destroy their supply must have worked better than he could have hoped. It was a stroke of luck that last night's storm had not brought rain.

Jake and Alison did not go into the sycamores. They halted across the dry stream bed. Jake motioned Alison to cover; then, from behind the protection of a large boulder, he leveled his carbine at de Lacey and Whip.

Whip was furious. He looked naked without his revolver and belt. He couldn't keep his hands still; he didn't seem to know where to put them.

De Lacey showed no emotion. He bowed stiffly, without his usual fluid grace. "*Bon jour*, Colonel. *Bon jour, Mademoiselle* Alison." His words were slurred because of his swollen tongue. If he suspected what had passed between Jake and Alison, he did not say it. "You are faring well, *mademoiselle?*"

"I'm alive," said Alison. She pointed her pistol at him coolly.

Jake forced a grin. "Hello, de Lacey. Figured we'd be seeing you again."

"Forgive us for not arriving sooner," de Lacey said. "It was my intention to take you last night, but the storm held us up. We knew you were camped nearby, but we weren't sure where. Poor Wabash must have stumbled onto you by accident."

"Where's Skeggs?" said Jake.

The handsome Frenchman's smile shone whitely through his dark whiskers. It was a painful smile, though, because his lips were bleeding. "Mr. Skeggs and I had a difference of opinion. Unfortunately for him, the—ah— thrust . . . of my argument was rather more effective than his."

"So Whip's your right-hand man now, eh?"

"You'll find out what kind of man I am soon enough, Moran," snarled Whip. Whip's fingers were long, like an artist's. They flexed and unflexed, as if longing for the feel of his absent pistol.

All this time, the barrel of Jake's carbine was pointed midway between de Lacey and Whip. The hammer was back. A touch of the wrist, and Jake could kill either man. De Lacey made a show of displaying hurt feelings. "You disappoint me, Colonel. You have not come in good faith. Mr. Whip and I are unarmed."

"That's your mistake," Jake told him. "Say what you come to say, de Lacey. Try anything funny, and you'll get what Wabash got."

De Lacey hesitated, then smiled broadly, like a practical joker whose trick has been discovered. He nodded to Whip. Slowly, so as not to get himself shot. Whip took off his hat. He waved the hat over his head twice, staring at Jake with hatred.

* * *

Across the canyon, three of de Lacey's men watched Whip's gesture.

"Stop!" said Davey Whip. "That's the sign not to shoot!"

Reese halted his finger on the trigger of his Sharps rifle.

"Christ," rasped Angel. "Shoot the bastards anyway, will you, Reese? Let's be done with it." Long-haired Angel was no longer interested in Moran or the woman; he was no longer interested in the treasure. All he could see was the spring atop that rise. All he could think about was water. "Go ahead—shoot them and we can get a drink. I'd do it myself if I could hold a rifle." Angel's wounded arm hurt all the time now.

Reese's finger eased off the trigger. The ferocious-looking breed had sweated himself dry; he was panting. "I ain't got a good shot. Besides, what if I miss? Moran'll kill the boss, sure as hell."

"He'll kill my brother, too," said Davey Whip, and there was warning in his voice. Davey's nerves were on edge because of the heat and thirst and the danger his brother was in. "De Lacey says don't shoot, and that's what we'll do."

Angel and Reese didn't challenge him; they were too scared of his brother. Davey had another reason for not wanting Moran shot. Ever since they had found Hammond's body, and he realized he could not get his revenge on the boy, Davey had been thinking of bigger things—like killing Moran himself. He could do it. He was good with a gun, maybe better than Denny, if they put it to a test. Why leave Moran and the glory for his brother? Why not build his own reputation?

The two remaining members of de Lacey's party were off by themselves. They had seen Whip's signal, too, and obeyed. Nine-Finger Charley sat motionless, nearly invisible behind a screen of rock and brush. His rifle was cradled in his arms. He sucked pebbles to ward off thirst, as his Apache mother had taught him. He did not like being here. This canyon was sacred; it was the home of a Mountain Spirit. Charley had sprinkled pollen to the sun and the four points of the compass to protect himself from harm. He wanted only to leave.

The old *vaquero* Reyes was hunkered down in a strand of juniper pine, staring at the bleached bones at the base of the rise. He was thinking about a night in this same canyon, many years ago, when he had been a young soldier on sentry duty. He was thinking about the terror that had exploded that night, and how he had fled into the brush. There had been other survivors of the massacre. Some had died of wounds; others had drifted south to their homes, to the regiment. Reyes knew that the men who'd stolen the treasure had been attacked by Apaches. He believed that the treasure was still here in this canyon. He'd come back to look for it, to try to find this canyon again among the hundreds of canyons in southern Arizona. At first he had searched because he wanted to be rich, but after many years the search had become an end in itself, an attempt to recapture his lost youth. Yet he had always believed that God would return him here one day, and now He had.

Reyes said a prayer of thanks.

* * *

De Lacey said, "We want what we have always wanted—the treasure. I presume you have removed it to that house."

Across the dry stream bed, Jake answered, "Sorry, de Lacey, but there ain't no treasure. There was once, but it's gone."

"It's true," Alison said. "We went to the cave, but it was empty."

De Lacey did not believe them. His tone was impatient. "I am a fair man; my terms have not changed. Deliver the treasure to me and your lives will be spared. Otherwise, you will be killed."

De Lacey took his watch from his buckskin jacket and opened it. Despite his thirst, he managed to sound businesslike. "Ordinarily, I would not give you this chance. I would starve you out and take the gold at my leisure. With Apaches in the area, however, I do not enjoy that luxury. You have thirty minutes to decide."

"But we told you, there isn't any treasure," Alison cried.

Jake smiled grimly. "Let me tell you what I think, de Lacey. I think you're worried about Apaches, but you're more worried about water. I think you're more worried about water than about the treasure right now. The real reason you can't starve us out is that you and your men are dying of thirst. Well, you know where the water is. If you want it, come and get it."

De Lacey struggled to control himself. At one time he would have welcomed a fight, but now he desperately wanted to avoid one. He had not suffered from thirst this way since the Sonora expedition, and he'd nearly died then. Beside him, Dennis Whip clenched his fists. Whip wanted to kill Jake more than anything in the world, yet he lacked the means to do it. Jake's carbine held them both in mocking contempt.

De Lacey turned to Alison. "Perhaps you can make our friend see reason, *mademoiselle*."

Alison glanced at Jake, then said, "He sees what I see."

Jake felt a sudden chill, even though he was standing in the sun. It was time to go. He raised the carbine. "We're leaving now, de Lacey. You and Whip stay where you are till we're up the hill. Move, and you're dead." He motioned with his head. "All right, Alison."

As Alison moved off de Lacey looked at his watch once more. "Twenty-five minutes," he said icily.

Jake and Alison started back up the rise. Alison went first. Jake followed more slowly, covering the two outlaws with his carbine.

"Will there be a fight?" Alison asked.

"Sure will," said Jake, "and it's fixing to start any minute." He was unusually short of breath. He was getting colder and colder, when he should be hot.

Below him, de Lacey and Whip stood motionless. They would break for the trees as soon as they were out of range. Jake doubted he could hit them now; probably it was his reputation as the deadliest shot west of St. Louis that was keeping them in place this long.

Jake's chills became more pronounced. He felt nauseated. He blinked sweat from his eyes and he swore.

At a signal, de Lacey and Whip dove for the trees. Jake and Alison fired almost simultaneously. They both missed. Their fire was answered by a volley of shots from the opposite hillside, spattering around them.

"Run!" shouted Jake.

Alison scrambled up the hill. Jake struggled along behind her. He moved slowly. He was shaking violently now. He gritted his teeth, but, despite the danger, it was hard keeping his concentration. His mind wanted to drift. With a curious detachment, he heard bullets whine off the rocks and saw them kick up puffs of dirt. Above him, Alison fired her pistol.

"Don't waste ammunition," he heard himself crying. "You can't hit anything from here."

While he paused for breath she reached the top of the rise. She looked back. "Jake! Hurry!"

He waved her on. "Get under cover!"

He dragged himself upward, one step at a time, shivering. Bullets hummed around him; one clipped his hat brim. Somebody over there was a good shot. His feet slowed as if of their own volition, and there was nothing he could do about it. He wasn't going to make it.

Suddenly Alison was at his side. Her arm went through his, and she grabbed his waist. She began hauling him upward. "Come on."

"No, get out of here," Jake ordered.

Alison paid no attention. She struggled with her heavy burden, straining with the effort. As more shots sounded she made it to the top, half pulling, half pushing Jake over the crest of the rise.

"Hurry," she gasped. She guided Jake's faltering steps toward the ruined adobe in a flurry of rifle fire.

As she shoved Jake behind a wall, the gunfire died off. The canyon became suddenly quiet, except for the echoes.

Safe for the moment, Alison ran her hands over his body, feeling for blood. "Where are you shot?"

"I ain't shot," Jake told her. "My malaria's back."

Chapter 21

Alison looked at Jake shivering against the adobe wall. She did her best to appear unruffled. "You certainly have a theatrical sense of timing, Colonel. Am I expected to fight these men by myself?'

"If it wouldn't be too much trouble," Jake said. His teeth were chattering. He wrapped his arms around himself. He couldn't lift a pistol right now, much less fire it.

"We have my four Remingtons and that Dragoon Colt of yours," he said, "plus Wabash's Colt. That's six pistols and the Spencer repeater. Not much ammunition left, though. I'll take the two Colts. You unbuckle my holsters and put 'em on."

"I'll do no such thing," said Alison indignantly. "I'd look ridiculous wearing your pistols. I'll leave them in a—"

"Stop worrying about how you'll look! If you need them pistols, you'll need 'em in a hurry. You won't have time to go running around looking for them. Take the rifle, too."

Alison hesitated, then removed Jake's revolver belts and buckled them on, one around her waist and two across her chest, the way he wore them. "Jake Moran meets Hurricane Nell, " she muttered to herself.

"Make sure the guns are all full loaded," Jake added.

While Alison stuffed fresh cartridges into the butt-stock magazine of the Spencer carbine. Jake paused for breath. He was lightheaded. It was hard for him to keep his mind on what he wanted to say. The chills were already lessening. Soon would come fever.

They loaded the revolvers six shots to a cylinder, instead of five. It didn't matter if one went off accidentally now. Jake figured he and Alison would get shot up pretty good anyway. When the pistols were loaded, Jake said, "I figure de Lacey'll fake an attack from the left there, where it's open, and his real attack will come from the right, where the cottonwoods grow right up to the house. Behind them trees he can move in close and pick us off from cover. That's what I'd do, anyway."

"So how do we—or should I say how do *I*—respond?" said Alison.

"Don't waste ammunition, and shoot as many of the bastards as you can."

"You make it sound so easy," Alison said.

Jake was panting for breath. Sweat rolled from his hair. Alison felt his forehead; it was burning. She gave him some water from a canteen. Then she wet a handkerchief and tied it around his head.

Jake dragged himself to the crumbled right-hand wall. He rested the heavy Colts on a pile of adobe bricks, ready to fire. He sat against the wall, fighting to stay awake, fighting to stay lucid.

Alison stepped around the ruined ranch house. It didn't provide good cover. The wall was completely down on the right, halfway down on the left. There was a yawning gap where the front doorway had been. Only the rear wall, facing the spring, was reasonably solid, with a small doorway in it. Unfortunately, the rear was about the only direction from which they were safe. Alison had a good view of the rise, but she could see nothing of the hill that led up to it. The outlaws could emerge where they pleased on the rise's long crest.

She looked back at Jake. "What if we gave de Lacey the water? He could see for himself that we don't have the treasure. Is there no chance he would let us go?"

Jake was grim. "None at all," he said.

The morning sun shone with full force on the rise. It seemed as if they had been waiting much longer than thirty minutes. The outlaws might be approaching even now. Alison gripped the carbine tightly. She looked to the front, to the right and left, even to the rear occasionally, just to be sure.

The hot stillness of the canyon was suddenly shattered by de Lacey's cry. "Your time is over, *mes amis*. Give up, and we will let you go. You may even keep part of the treasure!"

Alison looked at Jake. His eyes were half shut, and his breath came in short spurts, as if he was trying to conserve his energy. "Are you going to answer him?" she said.

Jake shook his head weakly. "He's so smart, let him figure it out."

"Moran!" de Lacey's parched voice cried angrily. "Moran, answer me! *Mademoiselle* Alison!"

But Alison did not answer either. There was another silence, then de Lacey shouted, "Very well! Remember—it is your choice to die!"

He'd no sooner finished than there was a shot, and a bullet chunked into the adobe not far from where Alison was peering out.

She ducked back inside. More shots sounded from across the canyon. The lead slugs chipped the adobe and splintered the dry wood of the fallen roof beams. The fire was desultory, far from accurate at that distance, just enough to make them keep their heads down.

"They'll be coming now," said Jake. He picked up the Dragoon Colt. Beside him, on a blanket, he had boxes of .44 cartridges and percussion caps ready for loading.

Alison moved from side to side of the house, bent low, looking out anxiously. She'd almost grown used to the bullets hitting around her. She heard the horses neighing and stamping up at the spring, frightened by the noise.

She watched the trees to the right of the cabin, where Jake said the attack would come. Suddenly a volley of rifle and pistol fire erupted on her left. She ducked her head amid flying chips of adobe and went to the wall.

Reese, Angel, and tall Davey Whip were running forward in a line, spread out, firing as they came. Alison aimed at Whip. She fired once, twice, and the outlaws went to ground, shooting from behind rocks and folds in the earth. As they did, Jake croaked, "Here they come."

Alison moved to the right wall in time to see de Lacey and Dennis Whip break the cover of the rise.

Alison was in full view over the crumbled wall, but she didn't care. She began to fire at the two outlaws. Jake joined in with the Dragoon Colt. De Lacey and Whip stopped as bullets splintered the trees around them. They turned and scrambled back under cover of the crest.

Alison fumbled more shells into the carbine, cursing herself. She'd used a lot of ammunition, and she hadn't hit anybody. She'd never shot at a moving target, or any other kind of target, until a few days ago. There was no breeze, and the thick, acrid-smelling powder smoke made her eyes burn.

The outlaws on the left kept up a steady fire on the house. Now there were pistol shots from de Lacey and Dennis Whip on the right. An adobe chip sliced open Alison's cheek. She felt blood running down. She backed down into a corner, where she wouldn't be so exposed.

Suddenly—movement. The wounded, girlish-looking outlaw named Angel broke cover and began running for the spring. His comrades yelled for him to come back, but he didn't hear them. Thirst and the effort of climbing the hill must have driven him mad. If he made the trees, he would be safe. Alison stepped forward, trying to be calm though her heart was pounding. She drew a bead on Angel's moving back. She squeezed the trigger. There was a bang and a puff of smoke, and through it she saw Angel pitch onto his face.

"My God, I shot one," said Alison.

"It's about time," said Jake.

Alison knew she should feel revulsion at her act, but she didn't have time for feelings. Shots were hitting the adobe all around her. She was coughing from the smoke and dust. She tasted warm blood from her cheek and spat it out. She got a drink from the canteen, then moved back beside Jake.

De Lacey and Whip were moving closer, dodging from tree to tree, narrowing the range. Jake was trying to hold them off, but he couldn't hit anything with his shaking hands. Alison fired a shot at de Lacey. For a moment she thought she'd gotten him, then she saw him moving again.

She had exhausted the bullets for the carbine. She threw it down and began to use the pistols, moving from side to side of the house, stepping over saddles and roof beams and bits of gear. She was aware that the firing from across the canyon had stopped. The men who had been over there—Reyes and Charley and whoever else was left alive on de Lacey's side—must be moving closer.

Alison couldn't believe how many shots she'd fired without result—she must have used thirty from the pistols alone. The outlaws never gave her a good shot. They waited until she was preoccupied on one side, then they rushed closer on the other. They did not seem to lack for ammunition at all.

As Alison emptied each pistol, she passed the weapon to Jake to reload. He removed the cylinders. He put in the cartridges, seating them with the rammer. He wrenched off the used percussion caps and placed new ones on the nipples. He swore repeatedly as the copper caps slipped through his sweaty fingers.

"That's the last of them," he said, handing Alison a partially loaded weapon. They exchanged glances. Alison put the pistol in her back holster and turned away to fire. Jake tried to stand. He was trying to master the fever. Sweat poured out of him, and his vision was blurred.

Alison moved slowly now. Fire was pouring in on them from three directions at once—the other group of outlaws must have reached the crest of the rise. She was more tired than she could have thought possible. Her face and hands were black from powder smoke, smeared with blood from her cut cheek where she'd wiped away the sweat. No amount of water eased her thirst. The heat was incredible. She could imagine how bad it was for the men out there. She could imagine what had driven Angel to make his dash for the spring.

More shots drove her to the dirt floor. She gouged her foreleg on the edge of Jake's frying pan, and she bit back a cry. Her fingernails were torn and broken, her hands bloody from crawling over the rubble.

As Alison reached the left wall once more, she saw someone diving for cover quite close. Davey Whip. She snapped a shot at him that might have hit him. Where was the other one, the mean-looking one? Reese. She looked, didn't see him. Had he gotten around the side? Panicked, she ran to the front of the adobe. She got there just as Reese stepped over the crumbling wall.

He leaped forward, grabbing her. She was jarred. She pulled the trigger of her pistol. Nothing happened—the hammer was caught in Reese's billowing shirtsleeve. He had hold of her left arm, twisting it, hurting it. Crying,

Alison yanked the pistol. It came free from the shirt and fired. Reese staggered a bit. He laughed and came at her again. She fired—snap, the pistol was empty. Reese grabbed at her, his huge hands pinning her arm and waist. She battered his dark face with the empty pistol. He tried to grab her free hand, but she kept it away. Blood splattered his face. They spun around and fell to the floor. Reese landed across Alison's knee and she cried in pain. Then he got up and was pulling her to him. She dropped the revolver, reaching behind her back for another one. She pulled it from the holster, cocked it and pushed it into Reese's stomach. She pulled the trigger and there was a bang.

Reese's grip on Alison grew tighter. Then he groaned, loudly. He let go of her and slipped to his knees, still groaning. He held his stomach, and there was blood on his hands. He swayed and fell over heavily. There was a vacant look in his eye.

Alison bent over, gulping for breath. She knew she should not relax, but she couldn't help it. At that moment, Davey Whip stepped through the back door, holding his revolver before him.

Alison was helpless, too drained to lift her pistol. Whip hesitated; he was looking for Jake. Too late, he saw Jake standing along the wall to his right.

The Dragoon Colt was empty. Jake had drawn his bowie knife. Before Whip could turn, Jake stumbled forward and brought the knife down on the outlaw's gun hand. If Jake had been at full strength, the blade would have severed the hand. As it was, it sliced halfway through the wrist and became stuck in the bone.

Whip dropped the pistol, which went off, just missing Alison. He howled with pain. He gripped his arm and moved back out of the house. His agonized screams rent the air. Then he remembered where he was. He turned back to the house and, with his left hand, reached for his second pistol. But Jake had picked up the fallen weapon. He aimed it and shot Whip in the chest. The tall blond boy staggered and fell on his back outside the house.

Jake turned. Alison was staring at him. She had grown numb to horror. "Thank you," she gasped.

Jake wobbled, unsteady from fever. "No need for thanks. I'm getting used to this. I've shot more men in a week with you than I did in twenty years out here by myself."

"Why didn't you shoot him, then?" she said, indicating Reese.

"I was out of bullets. Besides, you looked like you were doing all right."

Jake rotated the cylinder of Whip's Navy Colt. "Only two shots left. Hell." He'd like to get the other Colt and Whip's cartridge belt, but he'd never make it across the open ground. "How many rounds you got?"

Alison looked. "One."

Fire was coming at them from four sides. Rifle fire, pistol fire—the outlaws had moved close to the house. Alison just wanted it to stop. Wherever they moved, someone had a good shot at them. Jake fired once more, and they withdrew into a corner of the wall, the last place where they were relatively safe. They sat down, wedged together as the bullets smacked around them.

"They'll come from all directions at once," Jake said. "We'll try to take two of them with us."

Alison's shoulder ached from the recoil of the Spencer. A trickle of blood flowed from her nose. She sniffed and wiped it away. Her thumb hurt so bad she couldn't use it. It took both her hands to pull back the heavy hammer of her revolver. Over the noise of the outlaws' guns, she said, "I suppose this doesn't qualify as hardship and danger in your book."

"It's beginning to," Jake admitted.

Alison cocked her head and looked at him. "If anyone had told me two months ago that I'd fall in love with a man who drinks a bottle of whiskey every day, with soap in it, I'd have said they were crazy."

They ducked as another volley of shots sprinkled adobe dust on them and sent chips and splinters whirring around the house. "Don't worry," Jake said. "The way our luck's running, nobody's ever going to find out about it."

Suddenly it grew quiet. It seemed strange not to hear the gunfire, and it took a minute before they realized it had stopped. Their ears still rang.

"What does it mean?" said Alison.

Jake twirled his revolver. He caught the hammer with his thumb and cocked it. "It means they're coming."

Chapter 22

De Lacey stood cautiously, a pistol in each hand. He stepped from behind a stunted cottonwood.

There had been no more shots from the ruined ranch house. De Lacey could see neither Moran nor the girl. They were either dead, out of ammunition, or preparing a last surprise—probably the last, if Jake Moran was involved.

De Lacey rubbed his tangled mustache with the back of his hand. His appetites were whetted. He had lost a lot of men, but that meant fewer men with whom to share the treasure; for, despite what Moran and the girl had said, de Lacey was certain the treasure was in that house. He should have enough men left to make it safely back to his ranch. It might be a good idea to lose Dennis Whip— and keep Whip's share of the treasure—once they were home. De Lacey would have no further need of the viperous gunman. Reyes and Nine-Finger Charley he would be generous with. They had been loyal to him, and, as a disloyal person himself, he appreciated loyalty in others.

Things had worked out well for de Lacey. He was rich, he was leaving Arizona, and he was going to have some sweet revenge before he went. Revenge that he'd owed Jake Moran for ten years. He would take revenge on the girl as well, but that would be a slower, infinitely more delectable revenge.

De Lacey's three surviving men waited for their leader's signal to move in. Dennis Whip could see his brother's body lying outside the ranch house. Whip sidled over to de Lacey, keeping his eyes on the house all the while, alert for any tricks from its occupants.

"I want Moran," he told de Lacey. "I want to make him pay for what he done to Davey."

"As you please," de Lacey said. He no longer cared who killed Moran, as long as Moran was killed. More and more, he was thinking about the girl. She had fought skillfully during the attack, and somehow that excited him.

De Lacey signaled with his pistol. The outlaws advanced on the house from all sides. They moved one step at a time, watching the adobe wall, ready to fire at the first sight of Moran or the girl. Boots crunched gravel. Whip's Petmecky spurs jingled. Birds chirped in the trees. The sun beat down.

At ten yards, de Lacey hung back. It would be prudent to let the others enter the house first.

Whip passed his brother's body. He was at the doorway, poised to enter, when a rifle shot sounded from above them in the hills. The bullet hit the old door frame, knocking loose a jagged splinter that ripped open Whip's forehead. His face was instantly masked by blood.

"I can't see!" he cried, obviously thinking he was permanently blinded. "I can't see!" He stumbled away from the house, clutching at his eyes.

Another shot rang out. Something zinged by de Lacey's ear and he threw himself to the ground.

While Whip ran blindly for the shelter of the crest; the others looked for their new tormentor. They saw drifting smoke on the hillside, but no figure.

Then they heard something. A distant cry—no, a laugh. The laugh was high-pitched, insane. It stood their hair on end.

The old *vaquero* Reyes heard the laugh and crossed himself. He was a simple man, and the sweat ran down his unshaven jowls.

Nine-Finger Charley gripped his lightning-fused amulet. He would not let it go. 'it is the Mountain Spirit," he said to himself. He turned to his friend Reyes. "It is the Mountain Spirit. I knew this would happen. We should not have come to this place."

Charley turned and started for the crest of the rise. He moved in a short-gaited Apache dog trot that was deceptively quick. Reyes hesitated, then followed his friend.

De Lacey was on his feet, raging, "Come back, you fools! Come back here, damn you!" They paid no attention. They were fleeing. "Cowards!"

De Lacey turned and stood before the ruined house. He faced the dreams of a lifetime. He was so close. But there were two guns in there. If they had ammunition, it would be death to go in by himself. He might kill one of them, but the other would most certainly kill him—if this apparition in the hills didn't shoot him first. He could not win.

He threw up his hands in disgust. Cursing in French, he turned on his heel and retreated.

* * *

Feverish, trembling, Jake looked around the adobe wall. A minute before, he had been waiting to die; now the outlaws were running away. It seemed like divine intervention. The outlaws were pursued by that grim laughter, like something from beyond the grave. Who the hell was up there? Jake shielded his eyes, but he couldn't see anybody.

"Take my field glasses," he told Alison. "See if you can spot him—or them."

Jake crossed the rise unsteadily, picking up Davey Whip's second Navy Colt on the way. The laughter died. There was nothing now but the hot canyon. By the time Jake reached the edge of the rise, three of the outlaws were heading down the canyon for their horses. Charley was first, followed by Reyes. Whip blundered along behind, using his shirt to staunch the flow of blood into his eyes.

De Lacey was still making his way down the hill. He held himself erect, contemptuous of danger. The game was up for him. By running from their superstitions, de Lacey's men had condemned themselves and their leader to a fate far worse than bullets, even a ghost's bullets, could provide. They were going to die of thirst.

De Lacey may have reached the same conclusion, for as he reached the dry stream bed at the bottom of the canyon, he stopped and looked up at the rise. He saw Jake watching him. The Frenchman just stood there, in the open. He was grinning, as if daring Jake to shoot at him, as if inviting it.

Jake took him up on the offer.

It was a long shot with a pistol, longer than the hundred-yard musketry courses they'd used in the Confederate Army. It would have to be quick, too—in Jake's weakened state he could not hold the pistol steady for long. It was the kind of shot that the Jake Moran of legend might make.

Jake cocked the revolver. He brought it up, held his breath and aimed, guessing at the windage.

He fired.

Down in the stream bed, de Lacey suddenly braced one leg behind him. as if staggering under a heavy weight. He stood straight again, but he seemed unsteady on his feet. He appeared to be laughing. He wobbled, then he stumbled forward and fell face down in the sand.

Chapter 23

The three surviving outlaws rode back under a flag of truce. Jake looked at the sun. It was going on noon. It seemed as if it should be much later.

The old *vaquero* Reyes dismounted and examined de Lacey's body, which was partly screened by the break of the stream bed. Reyes lifted his grizzled face to Jake on the rise. "*El Patron* is dead," he shouted.

Nine-Finger Charley touched something at his throat while he scanned the canyon nervously. Dennis Whip was behind Charley, glowering. Whip's forehead was bandaged now, and a lot of the blood had been cleaned from his face. Jake covered the outlaws with the second Navy Colt.

Reyes shouted to Jake again, "*Por favor, Coronel—* may we take his body? We are poor men, and *Dona* Altagracia will pay us to return it for Christian burial."

"Go ahead," said Jake. He was keeping his eyes on Whip, waiting for the slender gunman to try something.

Charley dismounted. He and Reyes lifted de Lacey's body and laid it across his saddle. While Charley tied the Frenchman's hands and feet together, Reyes called to Jake again. "One thing more, *Coronel. Par el amor de Dios,* give us water. We will die without it. Carlos and I never wanted to hurt you or the lady. We came here from loyalty to *Senor* de Lacey—he was very good to us. Now we only desire to leave this cursed place alive. We will never bother you again. I swear it."

"What about Whip?" Jake shouted back.

"*Senor* Whip will not trouble you either," Reyes said.

"How do I know that?"

"Because we have taken his pistol from him," said Nine-Finger Charley. Charley was in a hurry to be gone. "Without his pistol, this man is no more warrior than a woman."

Whip rode forward and looked at Charley angrily. Probably he'd shot men for saying less. Jake saw that Whip's holster and rifle scabbard were empty.

Jake called back to them. "Wait," he said.

He went back up the rise to the spring. When he returned, he had the canteens that Wabash had been carrying. They were a mixed bag—tin Army canteens, big wooden Mexican ones. Jake braced himself on an exposed pine root. One by one, he swung the canteens by their straps and threw them off the rise. "Here."

The canteens thumped to the sand. Reyes and Charley ran for them. Whip came, too. They unscrewed the canteen caps carefully and sipped the cool spring water—if they drank too fast in their condition, it could kill them.

"*Gracias, Coronel!*" cried Reyes. "*Gracias!*"

Jake motioned with the pistol. "Ride out."

The outlaws mounted and started down the canyon. Reyes led the horse with de Lacey's body. Probably they'd wrap the body before they got too far, as it would get plenty ripe in this heat. Charley led the horses of the dead outlaws—there were only three; they must have lost some animals on the trail.

Jake watched them go. He'd expected more fight from Whip. There was nothing Whip could do without his pistol, though. With a gun in his hand, he was one of the most dangerous men in Arizona. Without it, he was beneath notice. Jake felt sure that Reyes and Nine-Finger Charley would pick a quiet spot and kill the little Texan. They wouldn't want to be looking over their shoulders for him later, after he got another gun.

Jake hiked back to the adobe. That act took about all the strength he had left. His fever wasn't getting worse, but it wasn't getting better, either. There was no way he was going to sleep after this attack. Besides the unknown gunman in the hills, all this shooting was certain to attract Apaches, if there were any around. They had to get out of here. They'd take a wide swing and travel up the other side of the valley, so as not to overtake the retreating outlaws.

Alison was leaning against the crumbled doorway. She still had Jake's field glasses trained on the hillside. She'd taken off his gun belts—probably the first thing she'd done when the shooting stopped. She looked like an apparition. Her face and disheveled blond hair were streaked with black powder and blood. Her clothes were torn and filthy. Blood still dripped from the gash on her cheek. Jake knew he looked just as bad.

"See him?" Jake said.

"No. He's still up there. I'd have seen him, if he'd moved."

"Likely he's watching us, waiting to see what we do."

"Why did he save us?"

Jake shook his head. He didn't know.

"Is he an Indian?"

"Indian wouldn't mix in a white man's fight like this."

Alison turned her eyes from the field glasses. Incredulity crept into her voice. "Surely you don't believe it can be a . . . a . . ."

"A ghost?" said Jake. "No. No ghost ever born used a Sharps carbine. I don't know who it is, and frankly I ain't sticking around long enough to find out."

"Well, I am," said Alison. She handed the field glasses to Jake.

"Where are you going?"

"To find him, of course."

Jake grabbed Alison's arm. "Are you crazy? He's as likely to shoot you as he is anybody else. We have to get out—"

"I don't think so." Alison pulled away. "There's something in me. I—I can't explain it. I just have to know. He saved our lives."

Alison crossed the rise. "Come back!" Jake cried.

She paid no heed. She passed the spring and started working her way up the canyon's side. Jake couldn't go after her—not now, anyway. He was beat hollow. He had to get some strength back. He poured more water on the handkerchief and retied it around his feverish head, like a pirate. For the moment, all he could do was lift his field glasses and watch the spot where the gunsmoke had appeared.

Higher and higher Alison climbed. It was hard going. Her right knee—the one Reese had fallen on—hurt badly. There was blood in her boot from her cut leg. She was tired, very tired. She was hot. Every bruise on her body throbbed. Why keep on? Why not let whoever it was alone? She did not know.

She must be close now. It was hard to tell; she couldn't be sure of the spot from this angle.

Below her, Jake's hands tightened on the field glasses. He was afraid Alison would be shot; he almost expected it. He should have stopped her somehow—held her down. She should flush out the fellow any minute. She was right on the spot, looking around. The man must have escaped. But how?

Something moved in the rocks Alison had just passed. A rabbit, probably. Jake looked closer. It moved again. It wasn't a rabbit.

"Alison—look out!"

She turned. Practically at her feet a man broke from cover. He started running through the rocks. He was bent over, with gray hair. He looked like an Indian.

Alison recovered from the initial shock and scrambled after the man. He moved fast for someone so old. He was carrying a rifle. "Wait!" she cried. "I just want to talk to you!"

She followed the old Indian up the canyon's side, around a bend. She tripped and fell, cutting her hands and knees. They'd been cut many times that day; now the lacerated flesh was ripped again. She picked herself up and kept going.

"Wait!"

The man dropped into a hollow. Alison followed him, sliding down the side of the depression, bracing herself with her torn hands, trying to ignore the pain. She stood at the bottom. She didn't see the old Indian. Where had he gone? For the first time she wished she'd brought a pistol.

"I want to talk!" she cried.

She paused for breath by a towering boulder. The air was still, ominous. Alison was scared now. She had started to back up when the old man leaped at her from the other side of the boulder. He pinned her to the ground with surprising strength. His knees pressed her shoulders; rocks dug into her back. The old man had a gagging stench to him. He was not Indian; he was white. He had thin hair and a square jaw with a long beard. All the bones on the left side of his face had once been broken—it looked as if his head had been caved in.

Snarling like an animal, the misshapen old man held a knife above Alison's throat. He prepared to plunge it home.

"Don't," cried Alison. "Please don't!"

He stopped, but not because of her pleas. He leaned forward and his mad eyes peered closely at her. Then he backed away, lowering the knife. His tanned face went chalky white, as if he'd seen someone rise from the grave.

He searched the forgotten recesses of his mind, flapping one hand rapidly as if that would speed his thought processes. He looked at her again, and the words seemed to speak themselves.

"Tom," he said. "Tom Shaw."

Chapter 24

The misshapen old man got off Alison. He was staring, his head cocked. He kept his right eye toward Alison; she guessed the left had been damaged by the blow that had caved in his head. He looked befuddled, and his words came slowly, no doubt because he was out of practice speaking. "You be the image of Tom Shaw. But . . . but you be a . . . you be a woman."

Alison found herself fighting for breath. Her head rang. She'd often been told she resembled her father. "I— I'm Thomas Shaw's daughter, Alison. Who are you?"

"Daughter?" said the old man. His thick gray eyebrows knit. "Tom never said he had no daughter. You look older'n him, anyway. Be a sister, mebbe." The old man was dressed in scraps of clothing that he had acquired or made over the years—a vest that had once complemented someone's suit, a dark velvet loincloth, an Indian's calico headband. His few remaining teeth were greenish brown, and they looked especially large because his gums had receded so. There was a vile growth on the back of his left arm.

Alison sat up, rubbing her shoulders where he'd been kneeling on them. "I'm Tom Shaw's daughter. Why would I lie about something like that?"

The old man had no answer. He had no choice but to believe her. He twitched his head, puzzled.

Alison struggled to her feet. "Who are you?" she repeated. "And how do you know my father?"

"Who am I?" The old man tried to remember. He hadn't heard his name spoken in many years. He'd nearly forgotten it.

"Det . . ." he began. He shook his head—that wasn't right.

"Den. . . ." He nodded to himself; that was better. "Den-ton." Yes, that was it. "Den-ton. Harry Den-ton. Me." His face was lit with accomplishment.

Alison gasped, "My Lord. Harry Denton. It's impossible." She tried to reconcile this shriveled, cruelly disfigured old man with the sturdy frontiersman that her father's letter had portrayed. It was impossible, but it was true. "My—my father thought you were killed. He saw it happen."

The bearded old man leaned in close to her and winked. His breath was overpowering. "Take more'n an Apache war club to kill me. Got a hard head, has Harry Denton." He capered grotesquely and grinned his near-toothless grin. "Tom's a good boy. Best of us all. Should have knowed he'd get away. Why didn't he come back hisself?"

"My father is dead," Alison explained. "He left me a letter telling me about the treasure, about what happened to your party. He left me a map."

Denton did not want to talk about the treasure. "Didn't know Tom had no daughter. Don't see how you could be so growed up."

"He didn't have a daughter then. That was twenty-nine years ago."

There was a blank look in the old man's eyes. He chewed his lip. Alison realized the truth. "You don't know how long you've been here, do you?"

"Long? Not so long. I'm going home soon."

"Soon? It's 1866, Mr. Denton. There's been a war with Mexico, and a civil war, and the slaves are free, and they're building a railroad to California, and . . ." She stopped. These things meant nothing to this crazy old man. In his mind it was 1837. It always would be.

There was a clatter of stones, and Jake Moran came sliding into the hollow with two pistols drawn. "Alison, are you all right?"

Denton moved swiftly behind the boulder for his rifle. Alison said, "I'm fine, Jake. Put your guns away before there is an accident. Please."

Jake hesitated. Slowly, he holstered Whip's Navy Colts.

Denton came up with his rifle leveled, but Alison laid a hand on his arm. "It's all right, Mr. Denton. This is a friend." It was like soothing a child; like soothing Hammond when he was small.

"Jake, this is Harry Denton, the same Mr. Denton who was with my father when the treasure was stolen. This is the ghost of Dead Man's Canyon."

* * *

201

Slowly, with many breaks, Harry Denton told Jake and Alison his story. When the Apaches had fallen on him, twenty-nine years before, they'd hit him so hard that they believed he was dead. They robbed everything on his body and moved on, chasing Tom Shaw. They did not return.

For days, Denton had been unable to move because of his injuries. He survived by sucking water from the pulp of a providential cactus. He ate ants and beetles. "Injuns like to eat bugs," he said, his head twitching. "Not me. Taste bitter, 'specially when you eat 'em raw. Know what I done? Made me a snare. Caught me a black-tailed rabbit, skinned him with a sharp rock. Much better."

Denton did not know how many days he had lain in the open. The buzzards used to land and sit near him, he remembered, watching him, and he talked to them. When he was able to move, he'd crawled away to shelter. Since that time, he'd never left the canyon. "This canyon is mine. Anybody comes here, I know what to do with him. That house down there—I killed some of the men who built it. Rest of 'em ran off. I pulled down that house with my own hands."

"What about the Apaches?" said Jake.

" 'Paches know about me. They tried to kill me, plenty of times. They never did, but I got me a bunch of them. Now they leave this canyon alone." He chuckled. "They think I'm Big Medicine, and mebbe I am. Head hurts. Hurts real bad, all the time. Must be some kinda spirits punishing me for my sins, don't you reckon?"

Alison turned away. She couldn't bear thinking about this old man's life—what it had been like all these years, what it might have been like had things worked out differently.

"Why didn't you kill us?" Jake asked.

"Oh, I was going to. Snuck right up on you. Then that storm come. After that, the other men. I decided to see what happened. That's why I was so far away when I started shooting. I was watching. Don't know why I helped you. Never done nothing like that before. Mebbe the spirits told me to. Yes, I believe that must have been it."

"Is that why you didn't shoot Alison when she came after you—because of the spirits?"

"Mebbe. Mebbe, too, 'cause she's a woman. Ain't seen a woman in . . . well, it seems like long while. Didn't seem right, shooting her. She kept chasin' me, though, so I turned on her. I never knowed she was Tom Shaw's daughter."

Jake went on. "You said you never left this canyon. What happened to the treasure? Did the Apaches get it?"

"Apaches!" The old man laughed and capered some more. "I got the treasure. Moved it from the spot where we hid it. Moved it real good, piece by piece. That's why you're here, ain't it—the treasure? Well, you're Tom Shaw's girl, and it's yours by rights," he said to Alison. He chuckled again. "Come on."

Chapter 25

Jake and Alison followed Harry Denton along the side of the canyon. For all his age and infirmities, Denton was surprisingly quick. In his moccasins he was like a mountain goat compared to Jake and Alison, who fell behind in their heavy boots, slipping and scrabbling for handholds on the loose shale. Weakened from the malaria. Jake dropped back behind Alison as well. After perhaps a quarter of an hour, Denton turned up a narrow side canyon. He climbed higher, then waited impatiently where a broken cliff face rose from the hillside in a jumble of brush.

Alison let Jake catch up to her. They approached the misshapen, bearded old man together. Jake was breathing heavily. His head swam; he didn't know if it was from the fever or what. He had to fight to stay awake. Alison's blue eyes drooped. They were bloodshot, but still looked unusually light in her powder-blackened face. The gash on her cheek was going to leave a scar.

"How much farther?" Jake asked, looking at the rugged hillside without anticipation.

"Farther?" Denton laughed gleefully. "We're here, my friend, we're here." It was the same demented laugh that Jake had heard earlier, and he didn't like it any better now.

Jake and Alison looked around. There were no tracks, nothing to indicate this area had ever been visited by man. Alison looked bewildered. Denton was still laughing, fixing them with his good eye. "Chose good, didn't I? That rock with the cross might have been found one day. This never will."

Denton bent low and slipped into the thick, head-high stand of brush at the foot of the cliff. "Come on, come on," he told them.

Jake and Alison followed him. The old man moved easily, bent double. He was used to this; he barely disturbed a twig. Jake pushed and hacked his way behind, tearing his clothes, cutting his scarred hands. There was no path that he could see. Alison followed him. Abruptly, the brush ended, and Denton led them into a zigzag fissure, one of hundreds in the broken cliff face.

The walls of the fissure were just wide enough to allow them passage. Jake and Alison inched their way along in the semi-darkness.

"It's an old Apache hiding place," Denton said from in front of them. "I found it by following them. They used it to store supplies for raiding parties. They could also lie up here when they was being chased. After a few of their parties disappeared, they stopped coming, and I took it for myself." He laughed again. "I took this whole canyon from the Apaches."

Jake saw a light ahead. The faint smell of wood smoke drifted down to him. There were other smells, too, fetid and dank, the smells of vermin and decaying food. Over- lying them all was the sour odor of unwashed man.

The light grew more pronounced. They crawled over a small ledge, and they were in Denton's cave. The chamber was long and low. A small fire burned in its center. The illumination came from a shaft of sunlight that streamed through a crevice in the rock ceiling. Beyond, glowing through the sunlight as through an opaque curtain, was the treasure.

Jake and Alison moved closer to it, drawn as if by an unseen hand. They passed the sunlight and stopped. Alison gasped; Jake's heart was racing.

The treasure glinted and sparkled in its shadowy depths like something with a life of its own, like a monster with a thousand eyes—of turquoise and rubies and pearls— and a body of gold, gold glowing hypnotically in the dim light. There were altar sticks and chalices; there was gold plate with the vice-regal seal. There were ceremonial Indian masks of solid gold. There were bejeweled goblets and bowls and knives. There were earrings and necklaces and brooches. This was wealth beyond anything that Jake or Alison had imagined possible.

"Pretty, ain't it?" said Denton.

"Overwhelming," murmured Alison.

"Didn't even know what it was when we got it. It was all wrapped in velvet. I took the velvet off. I like to look at it." Denton waved an arm that had once been brawny. "Take what you want. You're Tom Shaw's girl; you're entitled to his share. Ain't nobody to share it with now, 'cept me, so half of this is yours."

The old man chuckled. "Wanted nothing to do with the treasure, did Tom. He was the only one who spoke against taking it." Then his misshapen features grew serious. A faraway look came into his eyes, as if he had been allowed a moment of clarity. "Wish we'd all felt like him."

There was an awkward silence. Jake and Alison turned back to the treasure. Alison bent over a tarnished silver box containing rings of all descriptions. "Where could it have come from?" she said. "Where were those soldiers taking it?"

Harry Denton shook his head. "Don't know. Maybe the spirits sent it to test us."

"In a way, you might be right about the spirits," Jake said, kneeling. "Some of this obviously come from the Church. My guess is most of it did. Before Juarez come along, the Church was the only power in Mexico that would have had access to this kind of wealth." He turned over a set of heavy golden shoulder trappings fashioned in the shape of entwined snakes. It had taken a strong man to wear these. "Course, whether them soldiers stole it from the Church or whether the Church was sending it north for some reason, we'll never know."

Alison stepped back. She bit her lip and looked self-conscious. "Jake, I know it sounds funny, after all I've been through to get this treasure, but . . . now that I'm here, I don't know if I want it. I feel like I'd be committing a crime, like I'd be stealing. It doesn't seem right to take this."

Behind them, Denton stamped his foot and cackled, "Danged if you ain't Tom Shaw's girl, all right."

Jake got up, swearing. "Lady, I didn't bring you all this way to have you get cold feet at the end. We ain't stealing—and even if we were, that's what gold's for. Hell, the Church stole it from the Indians. Probably the Indians stole it from whoever lived in Mexico before them, and probably them people made slaves of somebody else to mine it."

Alison didn't know. "Your attitude seems so brazen."

"Damn right I'm brazen. I get half your share. If you don't take none of this stuff, I don't make a cent. I did my part—I got you here. Now you do your part and make me rich."

"Aye, lass," said Harry Denton, "you listen to your friend here. There's no curse on this gold, not anymore. The crime is paid for. It would be silly for you young folk to leave all this with me. Take it."

Alison took a deep breath. She agreed reluctantly, "All right."

Denton turned and busied himself with the fire, breaking a few sticks from a pile and placing them on it. "The spirits give me this fire. Started it with lightning. I never let it go out since. You want food, there's stewed rabbit over there."

Jake and Alison had forgotten how famished they were. They found some joints of cold rabbit meat sitting in an old mess tin. Denton must have boiled them yesterday evening while he'd been making plans to kill Jake and Alison in the adobe house. They sank their teeth into the stringy meat, ripping it from the bone, chewing with relish. All thoughts of decorum had vanished.

For the first time, Jake noticed the rest of Denton's cave. The walls were smoke blackened, but the lair was surprisingly neat. It was furnished with items Denton had found in his wanderings or taken from his victims. There were cookware and water gourds, a bed of moss and leaves sewn inside blankets. There was an evil-smelling bearskin coat for cold weather. Wrapped in velvet for protection, Denton's collection of rifles and pistols stood against one wall. By each were bundles of what must be cartridges and percussion caps. The supply of ammunition would be precious to the old man. There was a bow of mulberry wood that Denton had made himself, and an arrow quiver of mountain lion's skin. New arrow foreshafts lay near the fire, where they were being straightened. There was an assortment of tools, both metal and bone.

Near the ancient stew pot Jake saw a dog-eared, yellowing newspaper. He picked it up carefully, lest it fall apart at his touch. It was a quarterly, *De Bow's Review*, published in New Orleans in 1858.

Denton was watching him. "Used to be, I could have told you what all them letters meant. Can't do it no more. Still like to look on 'em, though. Don't know why."

One article caught Jake's eye. It was a passionate attempt by John J. Bowie to defend the reputation of his brother James. All the famous events were recounted—

Bowie's duels, the making of his knife, the battle of the San Saba. A coldness spread through Jake's stomach as he read. Twenty-two years after Jim Bowie's death at the Alamo, and people had still been arguing about his reputation—they were still arguing about it today, for that matter.

Was that how it would be with his own reputation? Jake wondered. A half-century from now, would men be debating whether Jake had killed Spotted Deer with a knife or a gun? Would they be writing scholarly articles, with footnotes, about his battle with the Colemans? It put a bitter taste in Jake's mouth. His excitement at finding the treasure began to fade.

"Jake, what's wrong?" Alison was staring at him with a worried frown. She had been drinking from a water gourd. "Is it your malaria?"

"No." said Jake, setting down the old paper. "It's nothing. I'm all right."

Alison motioned him closer. She spoke in a low whisper. "Jake, how do we get this old man out of here?" Jake watched Denton, who was humming tunelessly while holding one of the new arrow shafts over the fire, using a pair of iron tongs he'd gotten God knows where.

"We don't," Jake said.

"We have to return him to his people," said Alison. "With his share of the treasure, he'll be well off. Let him spend his last years in comfort."

"No. Leave him here."

"Jake, we can't."

210

"Even if his family was still alive, he wouldn't know them. He'd expect them to be like they was twenty-nine years ago. That Apache skull-buster addled his brains. He'll recollect some things perfect—mechanical things, like how to care for a rifle—and forget others. I seen it happen to fellows in the war. Besides, the world Harry Denton knew has disappeared. This is his home now; he wouldn't last a week anywhere else. Best thing we can do is leave the poor fellow in peace."

Alison looked down. Jake was right.

Jake was getting edgy. He wanted to get out of here. He didn't know why; it was just a feeling. "We'll never get half this treasure onto our horses. We'd need a pack train. We'll take small things, things that fit in our saddlebags." From a strong box he lifted a gold brooch in the shape of an Aztec cross, beautifully inlaid with emeralds and rubies. "Things like this. Alison, you pick them out. I'll saddle the horses and bring them up. I want to be out of this canyon by nightfall."

Jake left the cave. He fought his way through the brush until he emerged on the cliff side. Weary from fever and fatigue, he tramped back up the side canyon, pausing every few yards to turn and fix the position of the cave in his mind's eye. He reached the main canyon and climbed the rise. He passed the bodies of Wabash and Reese, of Davey Whip and Angel. Their deaths seemed to have happened long ago. He fed and saddled the horses, then filled their canteens and water bags from the spring. The dead outlaws didn't have enough .44 ammunition on them for his Remingtons, so he left two of them. He reloaded the Navy Colts and stuck them in his shoulder holsters. He stuck another Colt in his waistband. There was still a long ride ahead to Santa Fe, and you could never carry too many pistols when traveling in Apache country. He looked for Reese's rifle but couldn't find it.

Jake walked the horses back to the side canyon. His earlier excitement had died, and he almost wished they'd never found the treasure. His steps were leaden. The newspaper article had started him thinking, and now his soul knew the familiar feeling of emptiness.

He was going to be rich. Everything he'd ever wanted in life was within his reach, but he no longer cared. He felt hollow and . . . what? Guilty? Not exactly. Soiled somehow. Unworthy. Yes, that was it—unworthy. He was a failure—a failure with Hammond, a failure with Kurt Schankweiler, most of all a failure with Alison. His life was a record of failure. He was not deserving of riches, not deserving of good fortune. The Jake Moran of legend might have deserved these things; the real Jake Moran did not.

He reached the side canyon and looked up. The hillside was empty. Alison must still be in the cave. He yanked the horses' reins and started forward, heavy-hearted.

He would not keep any of the treasure for himself, he decided. He would do some good with it. He would give his share back to Alison. He would leave her in Santa Fe, and he would ride away. He would disappear into—

A volley of shots exploded above him. Bullets whizzed by. His horse staggered. He dropped the horses' reins and threw himself behind cover.

He pressed himself against the rocks. His pulse was racing. He eased the Remingtons from their holsters.

"Colonel Moran!" cried the suave voice of Edouard de Lacey. "Have we killed you?"

Chapter 26

"I'm still kicking," Jake called back. "Can't say I thought the same about you."

De Lacey's rich laughter floated down the hill. His voice was relaxed, cheerful. "To tell you the truth, Colonel, the idea of acting out my death was conceived on the spot. I played it brilliantly, don't you think? When your unknown ally joined the fight I was convinced of my defeat. Then I saw you take aim and I developed a *ruse de guerre*. I gambled that you were not quite the shot your reputation suggests. It was a stratagem to lure you into false confidence. It was not a brilliant stratagem—it was, perhaps, even stupid—but it was clever enough to fool you. You even gave us five canteens of the most enjoyable water. " He laughed again.

Jake snatched a look up at the cliff face. He saw de Lacey, with Dennis Whip alongside. No one else.

He ducked back behind the rock. "Is Alison all right?" he cried.

"Quite all right," came the Frenchman's voice. "For the moment."

Jake stiffened. "What about the old man?"

* * *

Up the hill, at the entrance to the cave, de Lacey was wiping blood from the blade of his long dueling knife, using a scented handkerchief. At de Lacey's feet lay Harry Denton. The old man was bruised and battered; he'd given the outlaws quite a fight. On his misshapen face was a look of surprise—the last emotion he'd known before de Lacey had slit his throat from behind. A pool of blood lapped the Frenchman's boot.

"My men are superstitious," de Lacey called in reply to Jake's question. He examined the knife blade, rubbing a stubborn stain with the handkerchief. "I wished to show them that a ghost bleeds like any other man."

Behind de Lacey, Alison struggled in the iron grip of Nine-Finger Charley. Charley had clamped his hand across Alison's mouth to keep her from crying out. The half-breed had followed Jake and Alison to the cliff face. He had watched there until Jake left the cave, revealing its entrance. He knew shame for having believed this crazy old man was a Mountain Spirit, and he was eager to prove himself further.

Nearby, Charley's friend Reyes looked grim. The old *vaquero* had seen his treasure again; he had touched it. His *patron*, *Senor* de Lacey, had brought him to this wondrous place. If *Senor* de Lacey wanted Jake Moran killed, Reyes was more than willing to assist.

Dennis Whip was next to de Lacey. Blood still leaked through the bandage on Whip's forehead. The Texan's jaw was set, his little eyes hard. He pulled his dark-barreled revolver. He checked it and returned it to its holster.

Jake's voice drifted up to them. "Let Alison go, de Lacey. You've got the treasure. What more do you want?"

De Lacey finished with the knife and sheathed it. This was his last handkerchief, so he did not throw it away. He would need it again soon. He looked at Alison and smiled. His white teeth sparkled in his handsome face as he shouted, "I want your life, Colonel. I want you to walk up this hill and put yourself in my power."

"And if I don't?"

Alison had ceased struggling in Charley's grip. Her blue eyes met de Lacey's, and they showed fear. De Lacey liked that. "If you do not surrender to me, I will have my way with *Mademoiselle* Alison. So will each of my men. After that, my Indian will strip the flesh from her lovely body inch by inch. Charley is not an artist like the late Mr. Skeggs, but his work will suffice—believe me, Colonel. You will hear her scream for hours."

Alison seemed rigid with fear. De Lacey kept smiling at her. He could wait to begin on her. Let her see Moran die first. Let her get a taste of what lay in store for her. That would make it better. She would fight then.

De Lacey had no intention of letting Alison live, but if he could take Moran by trickery, so much the better. He cried, "If you come, I swear to you her life will be spared. About your own life, I cannot in conscience be so sanguine. Now, Colonel—what is your choice?"

* * *

216

Jake shifted his back against the hard rock. His eyes were half closed. The hot sun beat down. The horses had run to the main canyon. The chestnut was shot in the chest; he would not be going any farther.

Jake felt tired and stupid, played for the fool that he was. How could he have believed he'd made a dead shot on de Lacey? At that range, with a shaking hand?

Jake had fallen for his own publicity. That was the biggest mistake he had made yet. For that mistake, he was going to die.

"Your answer, Colonel!"

Jake wiped a hand across his sweating face. He was under no illusions about the fate de Lacey had planned for him. He could escape if he chose. He could run down the canyon for Alison's horse. They would not be able to stop him. He could not leave Alison, though.

Should he give in to de Lacey? Should he pray the Frenchman had not lied about sparing Alison's life? Should he sacrifice his life on the hope of saving hers? Or should he try to rescue her?

What would the Jake Moran of legend do?

"I will not ask again, Colonel!"

All his life, Jake had been running away from his reputation. Now he must live up to it.

He squared his shoulders. "All right!" he cried. "I'm coming!"

Chapter 27

"Throw out your pistols," de Lacey ordered. "One at a time."

Jake unbuckled his revolver belts. He pitched four of the weapons onto the slope, where the men by Denton's cave could see them. He left the fifth pistol in his waistband, hidden behind his back. The outlaws did not know about the fifth gun; they would not be expecting it. They would see what they wanted to see—a defeated man sacrificing himself for a woman.

Jake stood. He started up the hill. This time he had no advantage. This time the outlaws had the drop on him. This time he was going to die.

He intended to take de Lacey with him.

He was banking on de Lacey's egotism to let him get close enough for one shot. The Frenchman wouldn't gun down Jake on the hillside; that was not his style. He'd want to make a show of killing Jake slowly; he'd want to impress Alison with his power. With de Lacey dead, maybe the others would let her go. That was Jake's hope. It wasn't much to hold on to, but it was something.

He saw them all now. Dennis Whip and de Lacey were closest, then Reyes, then Nine-Finger Charley holding Alison. They had Jake well covered. Probably he would have a couple bullets in him before he got off his first shot. There wouldn't be a second shot.

His footsteps grew heavy. They sounded loud in the quiet canyon. He was breathing hard, weak from the fever. He realized how much he loved life, how much he hated to leave it. The seconds seemed to drag on forever, yet at the same time they seemed to be flying by.

He was not afraid, not anymore. He was resigned to death. The way he'd been at Chapultapec, with the young Mexican soldiers sticking bayonets into him. The way he'd been during the dismounted assault on Fort Winfield Scott, running up the glacis into the mouths of the Yankee cannon. The way he'd been in Panama, wasted by fever and dysentery. This time, however, there would be no miracle to pull him through. This time his luck had run out.

Dennis Whip had been watching Jake intently. Now he started to come down the hill toward him. The slender Texan walked well out to Jake's side, his right hand just above his pistol butt. Whip's spurs jingled, and the silver conchos on his hat flashed in the sun. He was going to cover Jake from behind. He was going to make sure Jake pulled no tricks.

Jake's heart sank, and he missed a step. Whip would see the pistol at his back before he could get a good shot at de Lacey. He would have to deal with Whip first. He couldn't hope to outdraw the gunman, and Whip wouldn't be taken by surprise. There was only one possible ending to their encounter.

Jake had no chance to kill de Lacey now. Jake's death would mean nothing. Should he turn and run? Should he throw himself down the hillside, hoping to dodge the outlaws' bullets, and make for Alison's horse?

No. He could not abandon her. He must make an attempt to save her, even if it was hopeless. He had to go through with this. He must do it for Hammond's sake, if nothing else. He must die as gallantly as he wished he had lived. He held his head higher.

Alison's eyes were fixed on his. Her fear for him was plain. Gone was her cool demeanor. Her hair was wild, her clothing torn. Charley took his hand from her mouth, freeing himself to go for his pistol. He stepped to one side, ready.

Jake was drawing close to Whip. Another couple of steps, and the gunman would see the hide-out pistol. Jake made ready to draw. He had just a few seconds to live. The sun was so bright.

Suddenly Alison stepped forward and began to sing:

"Oh, if the ocean was whiskey and I was a duck,
I'd dive to the bottom and drink it all up."

Involuntarily, everyone turned and looked at her. "What the—?" said Whip.

This was Jake's chance. He pulled his revolver and cocked it. Whip realized his mistake and turned back, drawing his own weapon with lightning speed. Jake fired a fraction of a second earlier. Something tore through Jake's side. Across from him, Whip took a step back. Whip's thumb worked his gun hammer, but without effect. He swayed and pitched onto his face, and his hat with the silver conchos went rolling in the dust—but by then Jake was moving forward.

Alison had thrown herself on de Lacey, biting and scratching him. Jake looked for Reyes. Like his *patron*, the old *vaquero* had been surprised by Alison's move, and he was just now raising his rifle. Jake fired. Reyes fired, and his bullet skimmed a nearby rock. Jake fired again. The *vaquero* spun and sprawled on his back.

Two bullets left. De Lacey was still fighting with Alison. Nine-Finger Charley ran forward, firing at Jake, enraged at the death of his friend Reyes. Jake dropped to one knee, aimed, and shot the half-breed in the stomach. Charley cried out, stumbled, and fell.

That left de Lacey. The Frenchman had gotten Alison at arm's length. He smashed her with his fist, and she dropped to the ground. Then De Lacey turned to Jake. Rage contorted the Frenchman's handsome features. He fired in haste and missed. Jake squeezed off his last shot. Dust and buckskin kicked up from the top of de Lacey's shoulder. Not good enough. As the wounded Frenchman recovered and cocked his pistol, Jake sprang forward. There was a loud explosion in his ear, and he flung himself on de Lacey.

They went down together. De Lacey beat Jake with the pistol butt. He tried to lever the weapon into position for another shot. Jake grasped de Lacey's gun hand, keeping it away. They were on their knees. Jake twisted, and both men lost their balance, rolling further down the hillside.

Jake rose to his feet. De Lacey had lost the pistol, and his other pistol was up in the rocks somewhere. Jake rushed in. De Lacey braced and hit him on the jaw. Jake staggered. His head swam. Before he could recover, de Lacey hit him again. The jarring impact rattled Jake's brains. He was wobbling; his eyes would not focus. He was hit again, and he knew he would be killed unless he got a respite. As another blow smashed his ear he threw himself to the ground, rolling down the hill away from de Lacey. He came to his feet again, backing up, shaking his head, trying to get his legs steady beneath him.

De Lacey didn't come at him, not right away. He smiled at Jake, then he drew his long knife.

Jake's bowie knife was still in its scabbard. He pulled it out, eighteen inches of razor-sharp steel. He wiped sweat from his eyes with his grimy sleeve. His ankle throbbed; he must have twisted it. De Lacey came down the hillside to him. The Frenchman was balanced on the balls of his feet with his free hand held high. His expression was serious now.

De Lacey feinted and lunged. Stumbling backward, Jake barely parried the blow. He lost his balance, fell, and rolled over. He came to his knees as de Lacey lunged again. He scrambled aside and felt his left arm ripped open. He got up and came back swinging the bowie knife wildly. He'd never been in a knife fight, knew nothing about it. De Lacey easily skipped out of his way.

"Rather a poor effort. Colonel," said the Frenchman, grinning with amusement.

De Lacey flicked his blade forward, forward again, driving Jake back. He was toying with Jake now. Victory gleamed in his dark eyes. Jake parried another blow with a *cling* of steel. He swung his own blade and hit nothing but air. The Arkansas bowie knife was useless against the Frenchman. Jake's only chance was to get in close. He slashed and thrust, and de Lacey moved back, laughing. Jake didn't stop, though. He dropped the knife, lowered his shoulder, and ran full strength into the surprised Frenchman's knees.

Down the hill they rolled, all the way to the bottom of the draw, tearing clothes, battering muscle and bone. They were separated near the bottom. Jake was exhausted, the breath knocked from him. He wanted to lie where he was, but he knew he had to keep going. He lurched to his feet, looking around. De Lacey was on his hands and knees, reaching for the long knife. Jake flung himself on the Frenchman, dragging him away.

They fell. De Lacey drove an elbow into Jake's groin, and Jake lost his advantage. They grappled on the ground, gouging eyes, punching. De Lacey sank his teeth into Jake's ear, trying to rip off the lobe. Jake battered the Frenchman's nose with the heel of his hand. The nose broke; blood and gristle spurted. Jake got the stunned Frenchman in a firm grip and threw him down. As they fell, Jake's knee struck the sharp point of a rock. He yelled: a wave of pain paralyzed his body. His grip was loosened. De Lacey hammered Jake's torn ear, pushing him onto his back. The Frenchman picked up a rock and smashed it at Jake's head. Jake twisted; the rock just missed. It crunched the ground. De Lacey raised the rock again. Jake jabbed his knuckles into the Frenchman's windpipe. De Lacey gagged. Jake grabbed him by the hair and pulled him off, hitting his face.

De Lacey rolled. Both men came slowly to their knees. Jake swung a weary fist, but de Lacey dodged it. Jake lost his balance and de Lacey fell on him, grabbing his throat. The Frenchman's teeth were bared in his bloody face; his eyes were wide. Jake tried to break de Lacey's iron grip, but he could not. He was gasping, choking; he could feel his face going blue. His lungs burned for air; his eyes were darkening. He was dying.

With a last effort of concentration. Jake maneuvered one of his scarred hands behind de Lacey's head. He got the other hand on the Frenchman's chin. Images flashed through his mind—Kurt Schankweiler. Hammond. Alison. His brother, Ben, laughing. He willed forth all his strength. As his eyes went black, he snapped de Lacey's head hard right. There was a sickening crunch as the Frenchman's neck broke. He let out a strangled cry. The iron grip on Jake's throat relaxed, then it died, and de Lacey toppled off Jake to the ground.

Jake lay on his back, drained, sucking the sweet air into his lungs. Slowly his vision returned. His hands began to tremble. His guts were twisted. He could not put the sound of de Lacey's neck breaking from his mind. He rolled over onto his stomach, afraid he'd be sick.

He lay face down in the dirt. His body was a mass of bruises and cuts. There was a bullet wound in his side, and his left arm was torn open. What remained of his shirt was wet with blood. Aside from his knee, which felt as if someone had bored a hole in it, there was not much pain yet. That would come later.

He had won. He had beaten de Lacey. He'd never thought he had it in him. but he had done it—he and Alison.

Slowly he raised himself. Alison—what had happened to Alison? He staggered to his feet. "Alison?" Reeling around, he looked up the hill.

She stood by the cliff face, watching him. She was trembling and crying, because she was not alone. Around her stood close to a dozen Apaches. The Apaches were watching Jake, too.

Chapter 28

Tears rolled from Jake's eyes. After what they'd been through today, to be killed by Apaches. He almost laughed at the absurdity of it all.

The Apaches were quiet, waiting for him to move. There were more of them in the canyon and among the rocks of the hillside. They must have crept up while the white men were fighting each other. With their painted faces, they looked like avenging spirits come to purify their land.

There was no hope of escape. Jake was not thinking of escape, however. For once, he had no choice. For once, he knew what he had to do.

He had to kill Alison. He had to save her from their tortures. And when he had killed her, he had to kill himself.

He looked for de Lacey's knife. It lay a little way up the hill.

Instinct told him he'd never make it. He might kill Alison, but he wouldn't be able to pull that long blade from her body and use it on himself before the Apaches stopped him. He *had* to make it, though. He could not face torture. He could not face the pain, the screaming. Please, God. Please, not that. He had to make it.

He started back up the hill, limping on his injured knee, holding his wounded left side. He made his path come near de Lacey's knife. Then he staggered sideways and fell. He propped himself up, at the same time palming the knife. He rose again, slipping the knife inside his shirt, holding it against his side.

His head was swimming in the heat, and his body was starting to throb. Soon the pain would be intense. The Apaches fixed him with baleful eyes. They were an undemonstrative, almost nondescript people, it was their eyes that warned you what they were capable of. Jake remembered the crucified Mexican. He had to save Alison from that.

Alison looked afraid to take her eyes off him. Probably it was all she could do not to scream. Jake saw Harry Denton's body and its pool of congealing blood. Already the flies were swarming over it. The superstitious Apaches kept their distance from it. Probably the Apaches had seen de Lacey kill their enemy Denton. Now Jake had killed de Lacey. The Apaches wouldn't like that.

Jake was shaking, trying not to let it show. He'd never been this close to Apaches before without shooting at them. They smelled different from white men—a musty, feral smell. They wore war amulets in their hair and medicine cords across their naked chests, and their long breechclouts were tucked up for battle. A few wore blankets around their waists. They stood or squatted impassively, holding rifles and bows.

On the ledge in front of Alison, four of the Apaches consulted among themselves. One carried a shaman's medicine bag; the other three wore buckskin war caps.

Jake recognized one of the caps—beaded, with three golden eagle feathers sewn on top. This was the same bunch that had jumped them before. That tall chief might be Cochise. Gradually this chief's views gained preeminence, and as Jake came on the ledge the Indians reached a consensus. The council separated, and three members moved back, leaving Cochise—if that was who it was—by himself.

Cochise stood straight, rifle cradled in his left arm, right arm by his side. There were streaks of yellow, black, and red paint across his cheeks and a spot of yellow on his forehead. Up close, Jake could see that the war cap was painted with silhouettes of the gans, or Mountain Spirits. Cochise was a head taller than his fellows. He was well-built and handsome, with a long Roman nose. He had an aura about him, an aura of wisdom combined with savagery. An aura of danger. His eyes were mesmerizing. Jake could see why such a man was chief. He looked invincible.

Jake moved slowly, holding his side, afraid to meet Cochise's stern gaze. He prayed that de Lacey's knife didn't show through his torn shirt. The Apaches made no move to stop him. He reached Alison and put his free arm around her, as though to comfort her.

"You all right?" he said, trying to distract her attention. He slipped his other hand down the knife blade, to the hilt. He eyed the spot below her breastbone where he would plunge it in.

Alison was barely recognizable, with her powder-blackened face and hair, with the dried blood on her cheek. Her other cheek was swollen where de Lacey had struck her. In a low voice she said, "I have read that Apaches do not mistreat female prisoners, Colonel; so if that is a knife you have in your shirt, I suggest you use it on yourself."

"Knot-headed to the end, ain't you, lady?" Jake said. Grimly he added, "You also been reading the wrong books."

He braced his arms across her back. He gripped the knife hilt tightly. He tensed himself. He—

"Friend, you?" Cochise's voice was deep. With his rifle, he pointed at Denton's body.

Jake held the knife poised inside his shirt. He didn't know what Cochise's question meant, but the last thing he wanted was for these Apaches to think that he and Alison had been friends with Harry Denton, the ghost of Dead Man's Canyon.

"Friend, you?" Cochise motioned again, insistent.

Jake started to say no, but Alison spoke first. "Yes," she said. "Friend, me. Good friend. Friend, my father." Her head was thrust forward proudly.

"Hell," swore Jake. Now they were really in for it.

Cochise stepped back. The Indians consulted again. Again a decision was reached. Orders were given in a guttural tongue. Jake's hand was sweating on the knife handle. He had to strike now.

Cochise looked at Jake and at Alison. Then he nodded toward the bottom of the draw, where it met the main canyon.

Jake turned. A moment later, a bare-chested Apache appeared, leading Alison's white mare and another horse— Jake recognized de Lacey's black hunter.

It took a second for Jake to comprehend what was happening. "Christ," he breathed, "they're letting us go"

He eased the knife back inside his flannel shirt. "Come on," he said, taking Alison's arm. Under his breath he added, "Before they change their minds."

Jake didn't know Apache etiquette, so he bowed to Cochise, trying to look respectful but unafraid. He bowed to the rest of the council. Alison did the same.

They turned and started down the hill. They looked neither right nor left; they paused for neither weapons nor treasure. Jake did not even retrieve his hat. He helped Alison down the steep parts of the hill. He did his best to look calm—to look like he was on a stroll in the park—but his legs were shaking so badly he was afraid he would fall down.

Why had the Apaches done it?

Indians were crazy; everybody knew that. They could always be counted on to do the opposite of what you expected. That was what made them such dangerous enemies. "They must think Denton's magic protects us," Jake told Alison in a low voice. "They must think it would bring them bad luck to kill us."

"Nonsense," said Alison. "We were saved because that chief appreciates the truth, nothing more."

They reached the bottom of the draw. Jake's mouth burned with thirst, and his heart pounded with a strength he did not think it had left. He knew how easily

230

Indians changed their minds. He had to restrain himself from hurrying.

He took the horses' reins, forcing himself to ignore the Apache guard's intense stare. He helped Alison into the saddle, then he mounted himself, swinging up casually, as though he hadn't a care in the world. Without a word, he and Alison rode off.

* * *

Past the three buttes, past the entrance to Dead Man's Canyon, they halted. The westering sun threw long shadows across the land. The moon would be bright enough for them to travel tonight.

Jake was feeling the pain of his wounds now. Waves of nausea washed over him, and he fought them back. He had tied a rough bandage around his arm as they rode down the canyon, but the wound in his side was still uncovered. The bullet had passed between his ribs and out his back. Another fraction of an inch and it might have struck bone. It might have gone ricocheting through his body, smashing through muscle and vein. So little, the margin between life and death.

They dismounted, and Jake took off his bloodstained rag of a shirt. Alison cut away his undershirt with de Lacey's knife. She bathed Jake's wound with water and put on some medicinal cream. "We won't bandage it," she said. "The night air will do it good. We don't have clean cloth for bandages, anyway."

When she was finished, Jake lowered his arm and looked back at the canyon. Its interior was gloomy in the sunset. "We didn't map Denton's cave, you know. We'll never be able to find it again. The treasure's lost forever."

"Perhaps it's for the best," Alison said. "That treasure has never done anyone good—not my father, not Hammond, not Mr. Denton. I, for one, have no intention of going back for it. Let the Apaches keep it. It's their canyon."

She returned the tin of cream to her saddlebag, and her fingers touched something unfamiliar. She pulled it out. It was a small object, wrapped in dark velvet. She removed the velvet and uncovered a gold brooch, formed in the shape of an Aztec cross, inlaid with emeralds and rubies.

She looked at Jake questioningly.

Jake averted his gaze. "You wasn't supposed to find that," he said. "Not yet, anyways. It was for after— after we split up."

Alison made no reply.

Jake pursed his lips. "I wanted you to have it special. I put it in your saddlebag when I went for the horses. The value should get you home and see you safe for a while."

They stared at each other. Alison made no move.

"Look. Alison," Jake blurted, "about us splitting up. I—I ain't much at admitting mistakes, but. . . . Well, what if I said I was wrong last night? What if I asked you to . . . to . . . " His voice dropped off to a hopeless mumble.

"To reconsider going with you?" Alison said.

Jake nodded, chewing on the end of his mustache.

Alison put the brooch back in her saddlebag and mounted her horse. She looked at Jake and smiled. It was her first smile in a long time, and its warmth was equaled only by the sparkle in her blue eyes. "I had never considered doing anything else," she said. Then she added, "Well, don't just stand there. We have a long ride to California."

Jake grinned. He mounted beside her, and they rode away. They never looked back.

THE END

About the Author

Robert Broomall is the author of a number of published novels. Besides writing, his chief interests are travel and history, especially military history, the Old West, and the Middle Ages. He also likes to cook, much to the dismay of those who have to eat what he prepares.

Amazon author page:
https://www.amazon.com/author/robertbroomall

Facebook:
https://www.facebook.com/RobertBroomall.author

Made in the USA
Middletown, DE
12 September 2023

38395072R00136